DEMON MAGIC

Dragon's Gift: The Seeker Book 2

Linsey Hall

DEDICATION

To Bryant Bowler, the coolest Gamecock I know.

CHAPTER ONE

Bank of Lake Laberge
Yukon Territory, Canada

"I think I've got it." My magic finally sparked to life, a little ember shining inside my mind. Like a glowing orb, but so tiny and frail. I reached for it, envisioning myself with a hand outstretched to grasp it. The golden light of the magic warmed my fingertips.

So close. I reached harder, trying to control a power that was so new and unfamiliar. Honestly, I didn't have a clue what I was doing, but the visualization trick felt like it was actually working.

"You're doing well. The weather is turning," Roarke said.

My gaze darted to him. We stood on the bank of a lake in northern Canada with the sun shining brightly on the water's glass-smooth surface. Roarke stood closer to the shore, his dark gaze avid on the lake. For the hundredth time in the week since I'd met him, I was struck by how freaking handsome he was. You couldn't tell from looking at him that he was the Warden of the Underworld, the bossman of everything on that whole side of life, but it was clear he was one powerful supernatural.

I still wasn't sure what he was to me—we'd only kissed once and otherwise been as prickly as porcupines around each other—but he'd insisted on coming along while I practiced my new magic. He hadn't left my side since he'd learned I was one super weird supernatural. A SuperWeird, as I'd started thinking of myself.

But he'd barely spoken to me in the last few days—and he *clearly* had stuff on his mind that he wasn't sharing. Was it because I was a fugitive from his Underworld, and he was rethinking his promise not to force me to go back there?

I dragged my gaze from him. Now was not the time to be distracted by the fact that I had the hots for him. Especially since I had zero idea what we were to each other. He was helping me for now, so I'd take that at face value because I had bigger things on my plate. Like some seriously wiggly magic to try to control.

Raindrops sprinkled on my face. I grinned. The fair weather was turning foul, just as we'd hoped. My magic was working!

"Do you see it?" I squinted toward the lake, looking for the boat.

"Not yet. Keep going."

I may have been responsible for the rain, the weather turning worse by the second, but I wasn't a weather witch. Far from it.

I had a weird ability to bring the past back to life by weakening the barrier between the past and present. Problem was, I couldn't control it. I'd only had the power for little more than a week, and all it had done was cause trouble.

So, we'd come up here, to the middle of nowhere in the mountains of the Yukon Territory, so that I could practice going back to one specific point in time. It wasn't an important point in time, not to me at least, but it was more the specificity of it that mattered. We figured that being able to bring back the past from a specific moment was probably the most useful way to use my talent, so why not practice it? It was tough, but I'd always been a real *toss-me-into-the-deep-end* kind of girl.

"Come on," I muttered as I reached for my magic, envisioning the small steamboat *A.J. Goddard* puffing toward us through the storm. I knocked on my head for good luck.

And this wasn't just any storm. It was a storm from 1902.

In October of that fateful year, the little gold rush steamboat had encountered a storm on Lake Laberge and sunk to the bottom. It had happened only a hundred yards from shore. My goal was to bring that exact moment forward to the present, then send it back, returning everything to normal. It was the perfect tester, because there was no one to witness my forbidden magic out here in the middle of nowhere, yet the boat wrecked close enough to shore that I could see it happen, proving that I was learning to control my magic well enough to witness a specific moment in time.

It was genius, as long as I could actually do it.

Abruptly, the day turned dark. Rain pelted my face, and the wind picked up, roaring through the valley created by the rolling mountains. Waves kicked up on the lake, their tops glittering white in the dim light of the cloud-covered moon.

This was perfect shipwreck weather.

"Keep going," Roarke encouraged. "You're nearly there."

My muscles trembled with the strain of controlling my magic. I envisioned the steamboat puffing toward us, smoke billowing from its stack. A ping of magical connection zipped through my veins.

Suddenly, the boat was there, real as day, though hard to see through the gloom. I could even feel a connection to it, like I was linked to the past with a string.

Jackpot!

I squinted against the pouring rain, my heart thudding as the waves crashed over the bow of the little boat. I couldn't see the people yet, but they were on there. Five of them, if the newspapers were to be believed. I could feel a connection to them. To the scene that I had brought from the past.

But it was time to send them back.

Sweat prickled my cool skin as I reached for my magic, envisioning the historic scene disappearing back into the past.

Nothing happened. The wind continued to howl and the rain to pour. The boat struggled along as waves plowed into it. The smoke coming from the stack began to dissipate. They were losing their engines. This was it. Now that the boat had lost power, it would sink at any moment.

I sucked in a ragged breath and reached for my magic, but I couldn't get hold of it. The visualization trick of grabbing the glowing ball didn't work. I could *feel* my link to this scene from the past, like a wire stretched from me to the little boat. But I couldn't manipulate my magic enough to break the connection.

My heart thundered as my power spiraled out of control.

Could we be stuck in the past? Did I bring it back permanently?

A harsh sob escaped my chest as I pushed myself. I could do this, damn it! But doubt crept in as the small steamboat continued to flounder in the waves.

If I couldn't control my magic, how could I control anything at all? I was prophesied to be some kind of Guardian between the Underworld and this one, but I didn't know what the heck that meant. And what good was I like this?

A sickening sense of failure spread in my chest like a sickness. Too familiar.

Any grip that I had on my magic vanished, snapped like a broken wire. Or like a wall had slammed down between me and my magic.

"It's going down!" Roarke's deep voice carried over the wind.

He was right. It was sinking. Waves had swamped the deck and were filling the hold with water. Two figures grappled at the bow, then leapt into the water.

"No!" I darted toward the shore.

They would drown. Three had died in this wreck, according to old newspapers. I didn't want to let that happen again!

Right before I reached the water's edge, I felt Roarke's iron grip around my arm, jerking me to a halt.

"No!" His voice was harsh. "You can't. You know that."

"But…" I looked up at him through the rain, desperation making me frantic. "I can't just let them die."

"You must. We can't change history."

Disappointment carved a hole in my chest. I tried to tug my arm away from him, but didn't let go.

Because he was right. Changing history would be catastrophic. We knew that. Anyone who'd ever watched a TV show or read a book about changing the past knew that it ended poorly.

I turned back to the boat, which was nearly under now, sinking beneath the cold waves. I made myself watch, penance for my failure. I hadn't been able to close the wall between the past and the present, and this was the result. Witnessing this. Making it happen all over again. Making those men die all over again.

Without warning, magic swelled on the air. What the heck?

The ship and its occupants were human, so it wasn't coming from them. And the magical signature was nothing like Roarke's. His smelled of sandalwood and tasted of wine. This felt so cold it burned my skin and smelled of smog.

"Someone is here!" I whirled around to search the shore.

Two demons stood at the far edge of the pebble beach, near the trees. The shock of seeing them broke my connection with the past, as abruptly as if it had never been. It was annoying, frankly, how easily it happened when I wasn't trying to make it happen.

The rain halted, the storm returning to 1902, and present-day sunlight replaced the dark night. I didn't turn to look, but I'd guess that the boat and the crew were gone as well.

In the newly-returned sunlight, I caught a look of surprise on the demon's faces. One had the pale gray skin of what might be an ice demon species. The other was dark red. Fire demon?

"Where the hell did they come from?" Roarke asked.

Oh, this was just fabulous. First, my magic had failed. Now freaking demons were appearing out of nowhere.

Four more appeared at their sides, different species that I'd never seen before. Two with large horns, the others wiry as twigs. The horned demons held massive, curved swords that should have belonged to giants, while the skinny ones must have some kind of weaponized magic, otherwise they'd be armed, too.

One of the skinny ones wound up as if he were going to throw a baseball, then hurled a glowing green orb.

I ducked, the scent of sulphur burning my nose as it passed overhead.

"Acid blast," Roarke said.

Cold raced over my skin. I didn't want to get hit by one of those. They could eat through your flesh in seconds.

I glanced at Roarke briefly before calling upon my Phantom magic. It was still weird to shift around him— he'd only learned I was half-Phantom three days ago— but if I didn't want to lose a limb to the demon's acid blasts, it was a necessity. As a Phantom, I was faster, stronger, and most importantly, impervious to harm.

Shivery cold raced across my skin as the Phantom magic took hold, turning my limbs a transparent blue. Beside me, Roarke's magic filled the air. The taste of wine and the smell of sandalwood were followed by a mini tornado of black mist that obscured him as he shifted.

A second later, he burst into the air, his demon form a shimmering dark gray and his wings massive. In his shifted form, he was terrifying and beautiful. Against the pale blue sky, he looked like an angel of destruction. I grinned and pulled my sword free.

I, too, could be destruction.

Roarke swooped down on two of the acid blasting demons while I charged the rest. When the red demon threw a fireball at me, I ducked instinctively, even though it couldn't harm me in this form.

I leapt at one of the massive horned demons, not bothering to block his blow. His sword sailed through my middle, unable to make contact while I was in Phantom form. It was a creepy but handy talent. Unfortunately, I couldn't land a blow while in Phantom form. My ghostly sword would sail right through him.

Before the demon could recover his blow, I turned corporeal long enough to slice my blade across his neck. Warm blood spurted onto the rocky beach as I landed on the other side of him.

Blazing pain flared up my arm right before I could adopt my Phantom form again.

The fire demon! My knees weakened as the arm of my leather jacket melted. I sucked in a ragged breath, trying to ignore the pain, and turned into a Phantom. Once I'd shifted, my gaze darted across the beach, searching for the demon who had landed a blow while I was in solid form.

He stood about twenty yards away, winding up with another blast, his palm glowing red hot. Behind him stood the gray demon.

"You," the fire demon growled as he pointed at me.

Behind him, the other demon nodded.

"What the hell do you mean, me?" I demanded.

He growled again. I was going to have to be fast if I wanted to kill him without letting the fireball land while I was corporeal.

Wasn't gonna be easy.

I raced forward, sprinting across the pebble beach. Right before I reached the fire demon, Roarke swept out of the sky and yanked him up. He swooped away, taking him out to the lake and leaving just the pale gray demon behind. I grinned. Fighting with Roarke was efficient.

As the demon raised a hand to throw his magic, I charged. When I was about ten yards away, the demon hurtled a massive icicle. It was a glittering white spear that would pierce my belly like iron. I leapt out of the way, the ice missing me by inches, and nearly lost my footing on the pebble beach. I wobbled and righted myself, then raced toward him again, reaching the ice demon before he could charge up with another blast.

Instead of striking with my sword, I leapt upon the demon, taking him to the ground. I straddled him while in Phantom form, pinning him to the rocks. Though my sword couldn't cut while in Phantom form, I could manipulate things with my hands in my ghostly state. I thought it was because the sword was an object and didn't have the same magic that I did. Phantom magic was weird. And scary. Just by touching, I could make people relive their worst fears, sending them straight into nightmare and pain.

"Why did he say *you*?" I demanded. "Why are you here?"

The demon's face twisted as he thrashed underneath me. I didn't know how to control my power over his fears, but his eyes rolled in his head and he shrieked. Whatever he was reliving *sucked*.

"I'll let go if you tell me!" Actually, I'd kill him. But all that would do was send him back to his Underworld, a fate he likely wouldn't mind at this point.

"You're no Ubilaz demon," he rasped. "But you called us here."

My breath caught. I'd killed an Ubilaz demon four days ago by tearing out its soul, a power I hadn't realized I possessed. Ubilaz demons were horrible beasts that attracted other demons to them.

"What does that mean?"

He shuddered and his eyes rolled again, pain twisting his face at my touch.

"Tell me!"

"Must…kill abomination." He spat at me. It sailed right through me, but I still shuddered.

Gross. I scrubbed it off with my uninjured arm.

I shook him again. "Why?"

"Power stealer!" He spat again, then convulsed and lay still, captive to his horrible memories.

I would get no more information from him. I turned corporeal so that my sword would strike, then raised my blade and plunged it through his chest. As soon as my steel pierced his flesh, an icy electric shock ran up my arm from where I clutched his shoulder. The familiarity of the sensation made my stomach pitch.

This is what it had felt like to tear out the Ubilaz demon's soul.

I lunged back from the ice demon, heart pounding.

His soul followed, clinging to my hand as a wispy white smoke.

"Shit!" I stumbled and landed on my butt on the rocks. I flung my hand out, trying to shake his soul off. It flew away, disappearing on the wind. I shook my hand, which still tingled icily, and glanced around frantically.

All the demons were dead, their bodies slowly disappearing as they returned to the Underworld. Roarke landed on the beach, his boots thudding against the rocks. His massive gray wings folded behind his back as he approached. His magic allowed him to keep his boots and pants, though his shirt always disappeared to accommodate his wings.

I scrambled to my feet, my whole body trembling. The weirdest feeling was racing through my veins. It felt like they were full of antifreeze. I shook my hands, trying to make the feeling go away.

Ice blasted from my fingertips, frosting the rocks on the beach.

I jumped, my heart in my throat. "Shit!"

Roarke's eyes widened. "What the hell was that?" In his demon form, his voice sounded like gravel scraping together.

I stared at my hand, which looked normal. The ice in my veins had dissipated. I'd just thrown ice. Like Elsa. But I didn't have that power, and I wasn't about to start singing "Let It Go."

"I have no idea." The ground felt like it had fallen out from beneath me.

Besides being a Phantom halfbreed, I was also a FireSoul. We could steal other supernaturals' powers, but it was an intentional thing. I'd never done it before, but my friend Cass had. When FireSouls stole a power, it was a longer process that involved pressing both hands to another supernatural's chest as colorful flame enveloped your body. That was nothing like what had just happened with the ice demon.

Ice demon.

I turned to look at his body, which hadn't yet disappeared. It should have by now, shouldn't it?

"Del?" Roarke approached. "Why the hell can you suddenly throw ice?"

"Maybe I can't." I dragged my gaze from the demon's body and looked at Roarke. "Maybe it was a fluke."

"Try, then."

I nodded. My mind raced as I tried to process what had happened.

"Do it," Roarke said.

How though?

Try.

I closed my eyes and called upon my magic, poking around at my different gifts. I had so many new and weird talents that I was a bit of a mess when it came to using magic. But the signature of the ice burned cold inside me. It wasn't hard to find, and it was *definitely* there.

I reached for it, envisioning an ice spear. I flung out my hands toward the lake. Twin icicles shot from my palms, plunging into the water like harpoons.

"Whoa." I staggered backward. "That's new."

Roarke reached for my right hand, pulling it up to inspect it. I shivered at the warmth of his touch, then glanced back at the ice demon. It still hadn't disappeared.

"What's going on, Del?" Roarke murmured as he studied my palm.

I hadn't yet told him I was a FireSoul. He knew I was a Phantom and had some weird power over death—two magical talents which were expressly forbidden and could get me thrown in the Prison for Magical Miscreants—but the FireSoul secret wasn't mine alone. Since Cass and Nix were also FireSouls, I couldn't put them at risk by revealing my secret.

And that wasn't what had happened, anyway. I hadn't stolen that demon's powers with my FireSoul gift.

"I don't know," I said. "But we need to get out of here. I think those demons were drawn to me. We need to get back to my place where it's safe."

My apartment and the shop I ran with Cass and Nix were protected by charms that would keep demons out. I didn't want to hang out here any longer.

"Fine." Roarke started toward the ice demon's body. "But we're going to have to do something about this guy. He hasn't disappeared yet. He should have."

I glanced around. All the other bodies were gone. Whatever I'd done to him had made it so that he hadn't returned to the Underworld. Because he no longer had his soul? I shuddered.

"Put him in the lake." I begrudgingly pointed to the water, hating having to ask Roarke to do it. I liked to clean up my own messes. But I didn't have a handy pair of wings.

"That'll scare the hell out of some scuba divers."

"It's a mountain lake. The middle will be deeper than divers go. And the fish will eat him." Wow, how morbid was this? I felt like a mobster, knowing just how to dispose of a body.

"Fine." Roarke grabbed the demon by the collar and took off into the air, his powerful wings quickly carrying him to the middle of the lake. He dropped the demon and waited, no doubt watching to see if the body sank.

Some demons were denser than humans. I just hoped this one was.

By the time he returned, I was shaking from the cold.

"Did it sink?" I asked.

He nodded. "Ready to get out of here?"

"So ready." My arm hurt like hell, and the memory of the demon spit made me want to shower even though it hadn't landed.

I glanced at the lake where the body of the demon now rested near the wreck of the *A.J. Goddard*. Had this practice trip been a success?

Nope. Not really.

Sure, I'd brought the ship back. But it had all gone entirely to shit after that. Bringing the past back without being able to get rid of it was worse than not being able to bring it back at all.

"Ready?" Roarke held out a hand.

I eyed the icy water of Lake Laberge, shivering at the mere thought of it, then nodded and took his hand. He swept me up into his arms, carefully avoiding my burned arm. His muscles were tense, as if touching me were difficult for him. But my stupid heart raced as his warmth drove some of the chill from my veins. When he lunged into the sky, his wings carrying us high, it was all too easy to feel the strength of his arms.

I clung to him as he flew us out over the water. It glittered gray in the sunlight, calm once again.

One of Roarke's badass talents as Warden of the Underworld was that he could travel through the Underpath, a network of pathways that passed through the hells, connecting different places on Earth through portals. He could most easily access the Underpath through graveyards and haunted places. The wreck of the *A.J. Goddard* counted as both, which was another reason we'd chosen this place to practice.

The only inconvenience was that it was underwater. Only twenty-five feet deep, but still, that was an icy twenty-five feet to the portal entrance on the boat's deck.

"Ready?" His rough voice made me jerk my gaze upward to meet his eyes.

I nodded, then sucked in a breath and held it, bracing myself for the freezing chill of the water.

"Now." Roarke's voice made me snap my eyes closed.

I felt his muscles flex as he folded his wings, then we plummeted through the air, hitting the water with an icy blast. It was so cold that my head ached like the worst ice cream headache imaginable. We sank quickly, propelled by our fall.

Unable to help myself, I opened my eyes. The water glowed bright green. I leaned over to peer down, catching sight of the boat below. The bow loomed eerily in the water, a real ghost ship. The deck still intact, though the smokestack was gone, no doubt lost during the wreck. Machinery hulked at the stern. The engines, probably. At the very end was a massive paddlewheel.

The boat was in nearly perfect condition after all these years, down to the pair of old leather boots sitting in the mud next to the hull. Thrown off by one of the men who'd jumped overboard to make it easier to swim? I shuddered, hoping he'd been one of the two to make it to shore.

We drifted through the icy water down to the deck. My lungs were burning from lack of air, and I clung to Roarke, grateful when I finally felt us stop sinking. Roarke's feet had hit the deck. He reached out a hand, and a portal glowed in front of us. We moved toward it, and a moment later, the crazy whirlwind pull of the Underpath sucked us in, and the world turned black.

CHAPTER TWO

A moment later, Roarke stepped out into the alley in the older part of Magic's Bend, Oregon. He set me down as quickly as possible and stepped away. I shivered when I lost his warmth.

Old buildings loomed on either side of us, and the late afternoon sun cast a golden glow on the cobblestone alleyway. Our clothes dripped cold water onto the stones. The tornado of black mist swirled around Roarke as he resumed his human form. Magic returned the shirt to his chest.

I shook my head, trying to clear it. "That's easily the weirdest form of travel."

"Let's get out of here."

I nodded gratefully and followed him out of the alley, keeping a wary eye on my surroundings. The ornate, colorful buildings of the historic district rose three stories tall on either side of the street. Supernaturals of all species roamed Magic's Bend, and though demons technically weren't allowed to leave the Underworld, they did. And this was the perfect place for them to blend.

They could be anywhere.

Were they really drawn to me?

I shivered again, as much from the stress as from the cold. I could handle myself against demons. No problem. But against a lot of them? When they ambushed me?

That was less certain.

Particularly if that weird soul thing happened every time I killed one. I did not want to be adopting all kinds of crazy powers. Especially demon powers.

We hurried across the street toward Roarke's sleek black car and climbed in. The fancy electric engine was silent as the grave as he pulled away from the curb, but the warm air blasted, making my muscles melt.

So much better than Scooter, my motorcycle. I loved Scooter, but he didn't boast heated air.

"I'm going to ask again. What the hell is going on?" Roarke navigated smoothly through traffic.

"I don't know."

"There are things you aren't telling me."

Yeah, duh. There were things I didn't tell a lot of people. Like the fact that I was a FireSoul. He knew enough of my secrets; he didn't need that one, too. Not until I could trust him. If I ever could.

"I really don't know what's going on." I rubbed my upper arms for warmth, wincing at the sting of the burn on my arm.

"How's your arm?"

"The usual." Hurt like hell. But that wasn't exactly unfamiliar territory for a mercenary.

Roarke pulled his cellphone from his pocket and punched in a number.

"That thing still works?" It should have gotten soaked in the lake.

"Magic." He raised it to his ear and spoke quickly, commanding someone to come meet us at Ancient Magic. Then he hung up.

"Who was that?"

"Healer." He turned onto Factory Row, the street that held my shop and apartment. "For that arm."

As Warden of the Underworld, Roarke had an endless stream of demon minions to do his bidding. One was a healer, which came in handy at times like these.

"Thanks." I didn't even want to look at the wound because I was pretty sure that the leather was melted to my skin. "You sure you don't have other things to be doing besides helping me out?"

His gaze landed on me briefly. "Even if I didn't like you, you're the most important thing to happen in Underworld developments since I became Warden. Not only did you escape hell after dying, you've got an unknown—and forbidden—connection to death magic. That makes you my highest priority."

"You like me?" Of course my dumb brain latched on to that part. I was *smooth*.

His mouth snapped shut, and he clammed up real quick, focusing on the road.

Yeah, that was more on par with the last few days. He might have kissed me a few days ago, but he'd barely spoken to me since then. What the heck was going on with him?

I was used to a more linear progression with guys. One kiss led to more kisses. Or if it was a bad kiss, the guy was out of there like the Road Runner after dropping an anvil on Wile E. Coyote's head.

But it hadn't been a bad kiss. It'd been a great kiss. And then…nothing. Back to business as usual, with Roarke still helping. Which made our situation as clear as mud. The lack of clarity sucked because I liked him, but the scary part was that he knew some of my most dangerous secrets. So I needed him on my side, and any kind of cool-down made me nervous.

"We need to figure out what the fact that you're the Guardian means," Roarke said. "And this new development with your powers and the demons only makes that harder. You're at risk until you can control your power."

It had been only four days since the Phantom dragon named Draka had told me I was the Guardian between the Underworld and this one. We still had no idea what that meant, and Draka had been extremely unhelpful since she'd disappeared right after dropping that bombshell.

He parked the car outside of Ancient Magic, right in a pool of light cast by one of the imitation gas lamps that were meant to give the street a historic feel. It worked, especially now that the sun was starting to set, casting the old factory buildings in shadow. If you got rid of the cars and Scooter, who was parked across the street, the place looked like it could still be in its heyday in the nineteenth century.

I climbed out of the car in front of Ancient Magic. The wide glass windows were dark. It wasn't even five o'clock, but it was close enough that it looked like Nix had closed up a bit early.

I shivered in the cool air, still wet from Lake Laberge, but I couldn't take my wet jacket off until the healer fixed up my arm. I'd rather be cold than pry the melted leather away from my burned skin.

"I'm headed to P & P." I turned and started down the street towards Potions & Pastilles, our favorite hangout place. "Cass and Nix will be there."

Roarke jogged to catch up, a small duffle bag clutched in his hand.

"Change of clothes?"

He nodded. "I've learned that I'll need them when I'm with you."

I grinned. "Smart."

A warm golden glow spilled out of the windows of P & P, welcoming me to my home away from home. I reached for the door, but Roarke's hand appeared over my head and pushed it open, holding it so that I could enter. I ducked inside the warm, coffee-scented space, some of my fear evaporating away at the sight of Cass and Nix seated in our usual spot—the corner with the comfy chairs. Together, we could handle this. Totally.

Right?

"What the heck happened to you?" Cass asked.

Nix's eyebrows shot up. "You look like hell."

"Feel like it, too." I approached the corner, weaving through the small, packed tables. It was Friday night, and as such, P & P was hopping with the weekend evening crowd. Connor and Claire, our friends who owned the place, sold whiskey and beer in the evenings.

Cass and Nix rose as I approached, concern on their faces. Aidan, Cass's shifter boyfriend, approached from the bar, carrying a couple of drinks. He was as tall as Roarke, but he looked friendlier. Still a bit scary, considering how powerful his magic was, but he didn't have Roarke's Underworld air.

Aidan's gaze dropped to my arm. "You all right?"

"Splendid."

"Need a healer?" He handed Cass a can of Pabst Blue Ribbon, her beer of choice, and passed a wine glass over to Nix.

Roarke joined me. "One is coming."

The door opened behind me and I turned. A small woman entered, clearly a demon from the sight of her two small horns.

"You've brought demons in my shop?" a voice asked from behind me.

I grinned, recognizing my friend Claire's British accent, and turned to see her approaching. Her apron covered ratty jeans and a T-shirt instead of her fighting leathers, which meant she was on P & P duty instead of demon-killing duty. She was a part-time mercenary like me and wouldn't take kindly to demons just wandering around. It was illegal for them to roam the earth freely, primarily because they were shit at keeping supernaturals' existence a secret from humans. Though it wasn't technically Claire's or my job to take care of random demons roaming the street—we worked on contract—

but us ignoring the demon was a bit like a doctor ignoring a heart attack victim.

"She's a healer," Roarke said. "Here on my authority."

I glanced around. Patrons were turning to look, but no one said anything. Roarke's voice carried, and even though these folks might not know he was Warden of the Underworld and it was technically within his rights to bring a demon here, it didn't matter. It was clear he had the matter under control and wasn't one to be messed with.

The small demon approached. Besides the tiny horns and the gray cast to her skin, she looked human. She even wore the flannel and jeans so common in this part of Oregon.

"What are we dealing with?" The tone of her voice was so deep that she sounded like the rumble of a truck's engine.

My brows shot up. Okay. So her similarity to humans ended with her looks.

Roarke nodded at me, and the demon turned to look, her expression inscrutable. Her magic glowed around her like a halo of pale gray light. She approached.

"Thanks for coming," I said.

"Don't thank me yet." She nodded for me to raise my arm.

I grimaced and obliged, standing patiently while she hovered her hands over my arm. Her magic glowed brighter, and the pain flared, an uncomfortable reminder of my mortality despite the fact I could turn into a Phantom.

And come back from the dead.

So was I mortal?

A week ago, I'd escaped the Underworld after dying from a sword blow. That wasn't exactly normal.

After a moment, the pain faded. I risked a glance at my arm, relieved to see the reddened skin returning to its normal pale shade. The burned leather flaked off, drifting to the floor.

I met Claire's gaze. "Sorry about that."

She shrugged. "Floor's seen worse. You want something to eat? A drink?"

"The usual, please. You're an absolute lifesaver."

She grinned and headed to the kitchen.

The demon stepped back and dusted her hands off. "That's it. You're good to go."

I met her gray gaze. "Thank you."

She jerked her head back toward Roarke. "Thank him. I ain't cheap."

"Ah." I met his gaze. "Thanks."

He nodded, then looked at the demon. "Walk you out?"

"Yep." She followed him out the door.

As soon as he was out of earshot, Nix demanded, "So how's it going with him?"

"You asked me that this morning, right before I left. Nothing has changed. He's still distant. Doesn't talk much. Touches me only when necessary. But he sticks around to help. Makes me nervous."

"Stay nervous," Nix said. She was always the cautious one. "He knows what you are and is technically supposed to take you back to the Underworld. I know he's been helping you, but you've got to play it safe."

She was right. This wasn't just about me being moony over a guy I liked. It was a matter of my freedom and safety. If he wasn't such a huge potential threat, I wouldn't be so worried.

"Nah, he's cool. He's got a major thing for her." Cass hiked her thumb at me. "Hasn't left her side since she escaped the Underworld."

"That's his job," Nix said.

Cass turned to face Nix fully. "No, his job was to bring her back. But he didn't. He's letting her stay here."

Nix opened her mouth as if they were just getting started. I didn't have time for that.

"Guys, I have a problem."

Both their heads swiveled to look at me.

"I think I've stolen the Ubilaz demon's power." I pitched my voice low so the other patrons couldn't hear.

"What?" Cass nearly shrieked the word.

So much for keeping this quiet.

I gestured to the chairs. "Take a seat. Let's pretend we're normal."

We sat just as Claire returned with a slice of veggie quiche and a mug of boxed wine she kept especially for me.

I took them. "Thank you so much."

"No problem. Let me know if you need anything." She nodded back toward the bar. "I'll be busy with this group, but just shout."

I grinned and nodded as Cass and Nix leaned forward.

"Spill," Cass said.

I gazed forlornly at the quiche on my plate, then met her gaze. "So yeah, demons are following me like they follow the Ubilaz. One of them called me an abomination and a power stealer. He seemed pissed that I'd stolen the Ubilaz's power and wanted to kill me for it. And I may have stolen an ice demon's gift for throwing icicles."

Nix's brows jumped up. "You, uh, did the FireSoul thing? You sure that was smart?"

"I didn't mean to! I don't want to have a bunch of demons appearing on my ass."

"Yeah, that's not a handy power," Nix said.

I nodded. "Exactly. I don't *want* this. And when I took the demon's power, it didn't look the same as when Cass stole powers using her FireSoul gift. I didn't even try to do it, and it happened anyway."

Nix frowned. "How'd it happen?"

I explained how the soul seemed to get stuck to me when I killed the demon.

"Yeah, that sounds different than stealing powers with our FireSoul ability," Cass said. "It might be some combo of your death power and your FireSoul power."

"That's what I think. The first time I stole the Ubilaz demon's power, Draka helped me. This time, I did it on my own."

"So your power is growing," Cass said.

"Mutating, more like," Nix said.

"Great." I swigged the wine. "I'm a monster mash. Perfect."

"Hang on. Do you think that's why that group of demons showed up outside the shop yesterday?" Nix asked.

The memory flared, forgotten in my pain and stress. We'd been hanging out at our shop, doing inventory of our most recent acquisitions, when a group of demons had appeared outside on the street.

"I'd assumed they were just there to rob us, like normal," I said. "But yeah, now that you say it...possibly." I rubbed a hand wearily over my forehead.

Stealing other supernaturals' magic could make a Magica amazingly powerful. Unless it backfired. Like now.

The door to the cafe opened and Roarke returned, his clothes now clean and dry. Had he changed in the alley?

Resourceful.

I had a brief flash of myself hiding behind the dumpsters to take a peek and could feel my face flame red. For fate's sake, what was I turning into? I was embarrassed by my own brain.

He approached and handed me a warm sweater. "We need to get you out of those damp clothes."

"You wanna help her?" Cass asked with a grin.

I kicked her, not subtly, and met Roarke's gaze with an awkward smile. "We need to figure out what the heck is going on with these demons first."

He took the seat near me. "Any ideas?"

I tugged on his sweater, trying to ignore the sandalwood scent of it that made my heart race. How much truth should I tell? I was having a hard time trusting him, but I wanted him to trust me.

Anyway, he knew almost all of the story. The only secret I really wanted to keep was that we were FireSouls, since that one put my *deirfiúr* at risk. So I told him about unintentionally snatching the soul of the Ubilaz demon and our theory that I'd inherited his powers with it.

His gaze darkened with worry as I finished. "That's not good."

"Nope. I've got crazy new powers and no idea how to use them."

"You have to learn to control it. Then you can probably repress whatever power it is that attracts the other demons to you."

"Yes." I could feel the desire in my chest like a physical thing. "But I suck at controlling my power. You saw me back at the lake. It's like one moment I have control of it, and the next, a wall slams down in my mind, killing my control."

That familiar sickening sense of failure rose, suffocating the desire to learn control.

I sucked in a ragged breath and shoved it away.

I had to keep trying.

"Your new power could get you killed," Roarke said.

Great point. How was I supposed to be some great Guardian if I couldn't even survive my own powers?

Cass tugged a wide golden bracelet off her wrist and passed it to me. "Try it."

It was the one she wore to help dampen some of her powers. I took the dampener charm from her and slipped it on my arm.

"Now try to isolate the Ubilaz demon's power and repress it," Nix said.

I nodded, then set down my mug of wine and tried to identify the Ubilaz demon's power within me. I'd spent most of my life with only one power, so trying to figure out how to navigate the magical world with multiple powers was pretty weird. Every supernatural dealt with their powers differently, and most had been taught by their parents.

Not me. I had no idea who my parents were. Or if they were even *people*, considering what my weird powers were.

But I closed my eyes and gave it my best, focusing on my body and the magic that vibrated within me. I tried to envision them as different colored lights. The Ubilaz was an orange light, I decided. Not a nice one. A sickly orange. I tried to grasp it, but it felt slippery to my imagined touch. No matter how I tried, I couldn't get ahold of it.

"Does it feel like it's working?" Roarke asked.

"It's not," Cass said.

My eyes popped open to see her pointing out the window.

"We have visitors."

I turned to look out the window. Three demons had just appeared on the sidewalk, their eyes riveted to P & P.

Damn. I jumped to my feet.

This was my mess, so I'd clean it up.

The demons were muscle-bound lunks with massive horns and dark green skin. Their fangs were at least six inches long, and I'd bet my next paycheck that they dripped poison.

Customers turned to look at the demons, their brows raised. It wasn't the most unusual sight, so no one freaked out, but it still wasn't normal. Folks were on the alert.

Roarke stood beside me. "Let me take care of this. They're fugitives from the Underworld. My responsibility."

"I got it!" Claire called from the bar.

"No, I'll take care of it." I stepped forward.

"Seriously, let me." She grabbed a sword from beneath the counter. "This is my place, and I'll take care of it. Anyway, I'm itching for a fight."

"How about one each?" I drew the short sword from the sheath at my back and hurried to the door.

"No." Roarke's voice was low and firm. "Unless you want to collect another power, it'd be better if you didn't kill one."

Double damn. He was right. That added a whole separate layer of complexity to this nightmare. And I *hated* it. I cleaned up my own messes—especially if they were demons. But now?

I didn't want to steal that demon's power.

"Fine." The word tasted like dirt in my mouth. I stepped back.

Roarke headed to the door, but Claire beat him to it. She politely held the door open for him and said, "No one ever said we couldn't maintain our manners while sending demons back to hell."

I grinned, the first real smile I'd felt all day.

Roarke hurried onto the street, followed by Claire, and they made short work of the demons.

"This sucks," I muttered. I might have miserable control over my magic, but killing demons was my thing. I was *good* at it.

Now I couldn't even do that without possibly stealing their powers?

"You could try killing them remotely," Cass said. "I mean, it's something to consider. They're going to be after you, so you need a defense mechanism."

Like my Elsa powers. Shooting ice from my hand was remote. Even better, the weapon melted after it finished its grisly job. I'd just have to perfect its use.

"Good idea." I pulled the dampening charm off and handed it to her. "Thanks for the loan, but I don't think it worked."

She nodded as she took it, her green eyes riveted to the street, where evidence of the charm's failure was currently fighting our friends. Claire was wiping her blade off on a fallen demon's shirt, and Roarke had just broken the last demon's neck. His face was impassive, businesslike. It was clear that he didn't like the killing part of his job, but he was good at it.

But that would be my life if I didn't learn to control my power, which was growing and changing like crazy. Demons on my tail all the time and me relying on people to kill them for me.

The worst.

On the street, Roarke gestured to Claire and the door. She nodded and turned toward P & P, making her way inside.

"Thanks for handling that!" I called as I kept my gaze on Roarke.

He stood over the bodies, no doubt waiting for them to disappear back to the Underworld. They faded away to nothingness in record time, then he pulled his phone from his pocket and dialed. As he was talking, a sleek black car pulled up to the curb. I caught sight of the government license plate and my heart began to pound just as Cass cursed.

"Order of the Magica. Fuck." She glanced around, clearly considering bolting for it.

It wasn't a bad idea.

But the man was out of the car and nearly at the door in a heartbeat. Had Roarke called him? But no. Roarke was staring at his back, wariness on his face. He hadn't called the Magica.

"Just repress your signature," Nix said. "We'll be fine."

Cass nodded, her eyes still slightly wide. She was good at controlling her magical signature now, but her memory of being in the Order prison was still clearly front and center. Nix and I had always been good at keeping our species on the down-low, but even we got nervous around Order members and avoided them at all costs.

We all sat and tried to act casual, each of us focusing on keeping our magic tight to ourselves.

As the man walked into the cafe, his magic rolled out from him like a wave. His power smelled of the ocean and felt like vibrations against my skin. I shifted, uncomfortable and suddenly aware of my still-damp clothing. At least Roarke's sweater made me look normal.

We were sitting here, still as statues, and that was totally not normal.

I caught Cass's gaze and asked, "You want to see that new animated movie this weekend?"

Cass gave me the stink face—she wasn't a fan of cartoons like I was—then nodded. "Yeah, I could totally go watch a bunny cop beat up on some carnivores."

I kept the edge of my gaze on the Order member as he walked across the cafe. He glanced over at us, his bruiser's face out of place against his neatly tailored suit. Something like confusion—or suspicion—flashed in his eyes, and my skin chilled.

I rushed to make conversation. Act normal. "You'll love it."

My shoulders relaxed slightly when he kept on moving to the counter.

"I'm in." Nix raised her hand. "I love bunny cops."

Nix was like me—all for the cartoons. The guy talked to Claire as Nix recounted the basic plot of the movie. Though I strained to hear what he said, I got nothing. Just indistinct chatter.

But I did see Claire's face pale. She tried to play it off, but I couldn't tell if the Order guy bought it.

A moment later, Roarke stepped into the cafe, his long strides eating up the floor. He sat next to me, his gaze riveted to the back of the Order member.

"You know him?" I whispered.

He nodded once, sharply. "An Order Enforcer."

My throat dried. "Enforcer?"

"Yeah. Makes sure the rules are followed."

I knew what an Enforcer was. Anyone who broke the law—which I did just by existing—knew what an Enforcer was. As the man turned and left, I couldn't shake the chills. He glanced at us once more before leaving, that same weird expression on his face.

As soon as he was out the door, I asked Roarke, "He didn't recognize you?"

"No. Never met him. I only recognized him by the plates on his car. Enforcer plates end in EX."

Great. If he hadn't recognized Roarke, it would've been me getting his weird look.

Claire hurried toward us, her face pale. She sat in the seat nearest us and leaned in. "There's a problem. And it might have to do with you."

My stomach pitched. "Oh, fates."

"That was Orson Reyes, my handler—the one who gives me jobs on the Order's behalf."

"In person?" I only received assignments by phone or email. It was one of the perks of the job. But then, I was more part-time than Claire.

"It's a top priority case. Orson's a Sensor Mage with a specialty in demon magic. He's gotten wind of a disturbance in the demon power sphere. It's never happened before."

Sensor Mages were well hooked into the invisible magical power grid that overlaid earth. They could sense different types of power. If Orson could sense demon power, was that why he'd looked at me funny? Did he know I possessed some?

"What the hell do you mean?" Roarke asked.

"A demon has died, but his power hasn't disappeared from Earth. Orson thinks the demon's power may have been put into an artifact."

I nodded. That wasn't uncommon. Our whole business at Ancient Magic dealt with spells and magic that had been imbued into artifacts.

"He wants me to figure out what exactly is going on and take care of it. Orson doesn't like to get his hands dirty—that's why he's a handler and not a merc. But this way, he'd get credit with the Order for identifying and stopping the problem." Claire looked at Roarke. "I bet that's why they haven't contacted you yet."

Though Roarke was Warden of the Underworld and responsible for keeping the peace in the various heavens and hells, it wasn't his job to keep track of all the demons who escaped onto Earth. There were just too many—and most were small potatoes. The Order's mercenaries and bounty hunters—like me and Claire—usually took care of wayward demons. Roarke only handled the big guns. And this didn't sound like one of those.

Yet.

"So what's the deal?" I asked. "What does this have to do with me?"

"That's the problem. Orson thinks it's a Cat 5 demon's power that's running loose. An Ubilaz demon's power, specifically. He can sense that the demon is gone, but his power isn't." She glanced out the window to where the three demons had appeared only ten minutes ago. "And you're attracting demons, right? So I can only assume that Orson is wrong. The power isn't in an artifact. It's in you."

My heart plummeted to my stomach.

Damn, she was smart. I'd only just figured it out myself, and she'd put the pieces together without even hearing my whole story.

"Yeah, you're right." I reached up and pressed my fingers to the lucky pendant I wore. It soothed me a bit, though I really needed to get into my trove full of lucky objects if I wanted to feel one hundred percent better. It was my own version of Valium.

"It's particularly bad because only evil demons are attracted to the Ubilaz demon's power," Claire said. "That means that the worst of the worst are now acting unpredictably and weird."

Great. Just my luck.

"I have a little time," Claire added. "I'm obviously not going to turn you in. But you need to freaking fix this." She looked at Roarke. "Before they bring this to his attention."

The heart that had just sunk into my stomach rose back into my chest and started thundering. Holy fates, this was a serious rule break in Roarke's territory, something that he really didn't like.

Roarke nodded. "So if Del can control her magic and keep the demons from being attracted to her, Orson won't be able to sense the disturbance in the demon power sphere, is that correct? She'd then fall off the Order's radar."

"I think so, yeah," Claire said.

"Then that's what we have to do," Roarke said.

I gave him a small smile. "Okay. So I just have to learn how to control my powers while on the run from demons and the Order. No problem."

Except I had no freaking clue how to do that. So, big problem. Very big problem.

"I have an idea," Roarke said. "I have an acquaintance at Cambridge who might be able to help."

Cass's brows shot up. "The university in England? The all magic one?"

"They have an elite division of magical scholars whose life's work is dedicated to mastering the control of various forms of difficult magic." Roarke's gaze met mine. "Maybe they could help you."

"Wow, really?" I asked.

"I've never heard of that." Suspicion laced Nix's voice.

"No, they're secretive. The whole university is on lockdown, their various colleges operating independently and often in secret."

"I thought that was just because the town of Cambridge also has some mortals."

"It does," Roarke said. "It's one of the few mixed cities in the world. But the university is fully magic. That's one reason they're so secretive. The other is that they don't want everyone knowing exactly what they're up to."

"Then how do you know what they do, then?" Nix demanded.

Down girl, I wanted to whisper.

Roarke's expression closed off, as if there was a story he didn't want to tell. "Through my acquaintance."

"Then we'll come with you," Nix said. "The way these demons keep showing up, Del needs the backup."

"She does," Roarke said. "But getting through the university and into my acquaintance's office is going to be tough. Normally, you need an appointment to enter. We don't have one. Cambridge is the Fort Knox of knowledge. To get in, we need stealth, not mass numbers."

"You couldn't just call your friend to get an appointment?" Nix asked.

"Acquaintance, not friend. And I tried, but he didn't pick up. I didn't expect him to, but I wanted to give it a shot."

"So you're heading into this Fort Knox with no idea if you'll even be welcome? To see a guy who's not even your friend?" Nix asked.

"I'll do it." I glared at Nix when she opened her mouth. "I have no control of this magic. And no idea how to even start. This is my best chance."

Who was I kidding? It was probably my only chance.

CHAPTER THREE

I showered and changed clothes in record time while Roarke grabbed a bite to eat at P & P. I traded my soaked T-shirt for one that I considered to be particularly lucky—a plain black one that I'd been wearing when a black cat had crossed my path. Contrary to some people's beliefs, black cats were lucky. Especially if they had a long tail. This cat had had a particularly long and glorious tail.

Ever since then, this had been a lucky shirt. One of many, since I made a point to collect them.

For good measure, I popped into my trove and grabbed another lucky pendant. It was a match for the one I was currently wearing—a black pearl that had been enchanted by a tree spirit that I'd met in Iceland a few years ago. Doubling up on pendants meant doubling up on luck, so I clipped it around my neck. It rested next to the other lucky necklace and my comms charm. Maybe it was a bit over the top to wear two lucky necklaces and a lucky shirt, but with what was ahead of me, I figured I was going to need it.

I was probably somewhere on the edge of being a hoarder, but I didn't figure I was there yet. Though I did try to show some self-control. If I let myself go wild with the lucky charms, I'd probably look like that little kid from the Christmas movie whose mom wrapped him up in the snowsuit and a million scarves. I'd be loaded down with pendants and charms and lucky this's and that's.

But for now, I was good.

With one last look at my colorful apartment, I tugged on a black leather jacket and slung my sword sheath over my back. It would have been great to get some potion bombs from Connor, whose mad skills with the cauldron made my fighting life so much easier, but he'd been out at a concert. None of the potions in his workshop were marked, and I sure as heck didn't want to get them confused. Number one rule in potions—know what you were slinging.

I grabbed the sweater I'd borrowed from Roarke off the back of the couch and barely resisted giving it a sniff to get a lungful of his wonderful scent.

When I got down to the street, Roarke was waiting for me at the car. He leaned against the sleek black body of the vehicle, two coffees clutched in his hands. A thin sweater clung to his muscles, and my heart raced at an embarrassing pace.

I forced my gaze to his and said, "One of those for me?"

"Yep. Espresso, just like you like it."

"Black as my soul?"

"Precisely." He grinned.

I loved that he kept up with my jokes. He handed me the coffee. I took it, my fingertips brushing his. He pulled away like I'd burned him, his gaze turning opaque.

Despite the heated looks he sometimes gave me, and our even hotter kiss, he didn't want to touch me if he could help it.

Frowning, I headed around to the passenger seat, sliding inside and tossing the borrowed sweater on the back seat as Roarke pulled away from the curb.

"So, do you have an Underpath that leads straight to Cambridge?" We'd use the same Underpath entrance we always did—the one in the alley next to Mad Mordecai's tea shop in the Historic District. But on the other end, I'd love it if we could just pop out right in Cambridge without having to rely on one of his demon chauffeurs. I really didn't want to see what one would do around me. Would it disobey Roarke's orders?

"Yes," Roarke said as he turned into the business district. Traffic was fierce since it was rush hour, and he weaved in and out of the other cars. "There's an Underpath in a haunted pub."

"Lots of pubs seem to be exits for your Underworld transpo-network. Why pubs?"

He shrugged. "They're all so old, with thousands of people passing through over the centuries, that they're usually haunted. Someone inevitably dies and doesn't want to leave the party."

Made sense. I glanced at him out of the corner of my eye, noting the controlled way he drove the car. Minimal movement, no jerking or speeding up too quickly. Certainly no slamming on the breaks.

Everything about Roarke was precise. Controlled.

Like how he hadn't kissed me since that first time four days ago.

Why was that?

Just the memory made my skin heat. It'd been the best kiss I'd ever had. He'd clearly wanted me. He'd even said he liked me. That I was special. Which, I'd admit, I liked. A heck of a lot. Who wouldn't?

But since then, he hadn't made a single move. Except to look at me. And boy, did he look. I could feel the heat of his gaze like fire. They weren't neutral glances. Nor even friendly.

He wanted me.

But he did *nothing* about it. Didn't even talk to me, really.

"So, how do you know this guy at Cambridge?" I asked, desperate to get my mind off the mystery of Roarke. "What exactly did he help you with?"

He glanced at me quickly, indecision on his face. "Something I couldn't do myself."

Talk about dodging the question. "Yeah, I know. How?"

I was prying, but I didn't care. I wanted something to prove I knew him. That I could trust him. That I wasn't being an idiot for liking him.

He sighed so quietly and briefly I almost didn't catch it. "Horatio, who we're going to see, was friends with someone I cared for. He tried to help him but couldn't."

"Your brother?"

"Oh, look, we're here." He pulled the car to the curb and turned it off, hopping out so quickly that one could assume the car was on fire.

So, looked like I wouldn't be getting answers to my questions any time soon. Roarke's secrets would stay his secrets. And it was damned hard to trust someone who kept so many.

It was damned hard, but I managed not to dwell on the fact that I, too, kept many secrets. If I was going to be a hypocrite, I wasn't going to think so hard on it.

I followed Roarke across the street, dodging a group of fae revelers. Their wings drooped slightly, a clear sign of fae drunkenness. We dodged them and continued on.

It wasn't late, but the party started early here in the Historic District. This part of town had the highest percentage of bars per street, so folks usually came here to party. P & P was where the hipsters went, the ones who wanted to play checkers while sipping old Scotch. The Historic District was where you went if you wanted to dance in bars while drinking dollar shots.

I liked both options.

Roarke led me into the alley, reaching for my hand as we neared the spot in the wall where the portal was hidden from all eyes but Roarke's. I gripped his hand tightly, not wanting to become separated. He'd made it clear how dangerous that could be.

Roarke squeezed back, making my heart speed up at the feel of his palm beneath mine.

No matter how much my conscious mind might be wary of him, my subconscious was ready to get aboard the Roarke train. Headed to Roarke & Me City, population: 2.

I snickered at my stupid humor, then glanced up at him to see him watching me with that same strange expression. His dark eyes were hot, but his hands were clenched in fists. Like he wanted to reach out and touch but didn't dare.

"Ready?" I demanded, annoyed with the mixed signals of hot eyes and cold behavior.

"Yeah." He tugged me forward gently. "Remember, don't let go."

"I know."

For good measure, he looped his arm over my head and wrapped it around my shoulder, making me shift my arm so that I could maintain my grip on his hand. I shivered at the heat of him against my side.

He reached for the wall, light glowing around his hand. Magic surged on the air, moving outward from his palm toward the wall. The familiar pale gray glow lit the wall, looking a bit like a passage.

We stepped in, darkness crashing around us as gravity disappeared. I clung to the feeling of Roarke at my side as my stomach plunged. The ether sucked us in, sending us on a rollercoaster through the blackness.

A moment later, we slowed. A door glowed in front of us, and Roarke pulled me through, then let go of me and stepped away as soon as physically possible. Like I burned him.

Only problem was that we walked straight into the middle of a rollicking bar fight. I shoved aside one guy who nearly flattened me, and Roarke stepped between two others.

"Settle down." His voice was deep and commanding.

The men immediately stopped fighting, but didn't look at Roarke. The enchantment that obscured activity around the Underpath entrance kept the men from realizing we'd just walked out of nowhere, but they'd still responded to the command in his voice.

With the fight settled, the pub was cozy, lit with Christmas lights that looked like they stayed up year round. It was late, probably past midnight, but the pub was still full of happy people. Two ghosts sat in the corner, visible only to me. They waved. I tried to ignore them, looking around the room instead. A fire blazed in the hearth, next to which sat a demon.

I blinked, then squinted.

Yep. A demon. He could pass for human, but something in his strange gaze—which was riveted on me—was clearly demon. Could I recognize him because of my Ubilaz powers?

This pub was full of supernaturals, but all of them passed for human, and there was no way a demon would be allowed in a place like this.

He stood, his eyes still trained on me, and stepped toward us. I turned my gaze straight ahead as we wove through the tables of patrons drinking pints of dark beer, but kept my senses alert in case he followed us.

It was snowing when we stepped outside, fat fluffy flakes falling on the historic street. I shivered and zipped my jacket. It was dead quiet out here—not a person to be seen on the entire street. Behind us, the buildings were Tudor, their distinct black timber and white plaster looking so perfect that you'd think it was Disney World's version of England. Except it was legit. On the other side of the street, the massive, ornate stone buildings of the university soared into the dark night. They looked like the fanciest old churches America could boast, with intricate stone architecture and ornate glass windows, but most were probably academic buildings.

I looked up at Roarke. "It's possible we're being followed."

"I noticed that." Roarke turned left and headed down the street at a fast pace.

I followed. "He was a demon, right? Even though he looked human?"

"Yeah." Roarke studied the university buildings as we hurried along. A tall wrought iron wall separated them from the street.

I glanced behind us, noting the demon stepping out of the pub and looking around. He was only ten yards behind and closing in fast.

There was nowhere I could go in the whole world that demons wouldn't perk up at the sight of me and follow.

I stopped and turned, meeting the demon head on.

"Abomination." Its voice was gravelly, its eyes trained on me as it reached for a dagger at its belt. "Power thief."

I swung back and punched him in the nose, following it up with a knee to the gut. He bent over, wheezing. I was about to draw my sword and go for the kill shot when I pulled up short.

I couldn't. Or I'd risk taking whatever power he had. Roarke joined me.

The words burned as I asked, "Will you finish him off? I don't want to take his powers."

The demon lunged for me, knife outstretched and nose pouring blood. Roarke grabbed him and swiftly broke his neck, then dropped the body.

"Thanks," I said.

"Any time." Roarke gestured to a section of the wrought iron wall. "We can go in here."

There was no gate. "We gonna jump over?" I stepped near and gasped. The electric prickle of a protection charm stung my skin.

"Not yet." Roarke stepped up to the wall, then drew back his fist and slammed it into the invisible wall created by the protection charm. Bright white lines radiated out from his fist as he tore through the ether, and the enchantment broke. The prickling that had bothered me disappeared. My muscles relaxed just slightly.

"Now we jump over." Roarke turned and cupped his hands low.

I stepped into them, and he hefted me up. I gripped the cold iron and pulled myself over.

With a heave, he tossed the demon's body over the wall, then jumped over.

"What'd you do that for?" I asked as he landed silently beside me.

"Don't want a human stumbling over him before he disappears. At least the campus is full of other supernaturals."

Good point. I turned to face the campus, gasping at the sight. It hadn't looked like this from the other side of the wall. Old-fashioned street lamps glittered with sparkly light. Magic light, not flame, like they were full of hundreds of fireflies. The light fell on the ornate old buildings, making them appear to glow. And though the snow gathered on the grass on either side of the walk, the pathways were clear and dry. Roses bloomed on bushes despite the freezing temperature. It gave the whole place an enchanted air.

The protection charm on the fence must have hidden the obvious signs of magic.

"Wow, maybe I should have studied harder." Or gone to school at all. The fact that I could even read was a miracle, considering the only parts of my childhood that I could remember took place in a freaking dungeon.

Roarke shoved the body behind a snow-covered rosebush and glanced up at me. "You could still study here if you wanted. You're smart enough."

A smile tugged at my mouth as I imagined the libraries that this place must have. They'd be huge and old and beautiful. I loved my trove full of books, but there was nothing like that feeling of discovery in libraries.

"Maybe."

"Definitely." His gaze was serious, but it moved away from mine quickly.

"How do we find your buddy?" I asked, determined to change the subject. It was hard to maintain any kind of objectivity around him when he was complimenting me.

"That's the thing," he said. "I've never been to his office. Just my, ah….friend."

He'd been about to say brother. I was sure of it.

"I do know that his college is somewhere in the middle of campus," he said. "The whole place is laid out as courtyards surrounded by buildings. Each is a college. A river that runs through the whole campus. I thought you could use your seeker sense to find it."

Nerves skated through me. Of course he wanted me to use my dragon sense on the fly, something I wasn't a huge fan of. I preferred to have my books to give me a boost.

"I can try." My gaze roved the campus, noting the many buildings and alleys and tiny areas. It was a freaking maze—and that was just the part I could see from here. "But info helps me. And I know almost nothing about this guy."

"I think he works at Boadica's College. It's dedicated to the pursuit of magical control. Horatio Penderren is a Mind Mage."

"A Mind Mage? What kind?" They could be dangerous. Each controlled a different portion of the mind. Those who could manipulate the thalamus, for example, could cause great pain for their enemies.

"He can manipulate people's self-control. Which means he could help you manage your magic."

"Makes sense. Well, let me try."

I closed my eyes and focused on what I knew, calling upon my dragon sense. The faintest quiver pulled at my middle, but not enough to get a target on where we were going. So I imagined how much I wanted to control this power. My dragon sense relied on desire as much as knowledge, so if I didn't know enough to find this guy, then I was going to focus on how danged much I wanted to find him.

Controlling my magic was the only way I'd survive. With these demons after me, and now with the Order on my tail, I needed to get a handle on my magic *fast*. The desire to control my power was so strong that I could almost taste it. I imagined it tasted like boxed Merlot.

It did the trick.

The familiar tug about my middle directed me into the campus and slightly north.

"I've got something." I set off down the path, momentarily pretending I was a student here. It was a lovely image, quickly replaced by the realization that I was hooked on my high-adrenaline lifestyle. I loved books, but I loved hunting treasure and demons just as much.

The thought of demons made me glance behind us to see if any followed. None did. But if someone saw us, would they realize we were intruders? I quickened my pace.

Roarke kept pace with me as we hurried by the ornate buildings, his gaze alert as he studied our surroundings. The deeper we walked into the university, the more obvious it became that this place was eight hundred years old. Lights glowed behind ancient, mullioned glass windows, shining on people bent over books. The feel of the magic grew stronger, too, varying signatures competing for dominance.

In addition to the usual Magica signatures, I got a whiff of fur and the feel of fangs nipping my skin.

"Do shifters study here, too?" I asked.

"Yes."

The path we followed terminated at a massive wall of prickly green hedge. On either side loomed two tall, ancient buildings, their ornate stonework seeming to form eyes that glared down on us. There was nowhere to go but through the bushes or the buildings.

I called upon my dragon sense. It pulled toward the hedge. There was a small gap right in the middle.

"Twenty bucks that's a hedge maze."

"Not taking that bet. You're right."

"Let's go." I led the way in, following my dragon sense.

Inside, roses bloomed on the hedge walls. Snow crystalized their petals, but the scent was still rich. We were only a few feet in when the tall hedges cut out the light of the lamps that had dotted the main path. We had to rely upon moonlight, which there was precious little of. The snow clouds obscured most of its glow.

A moment later, glittering lights appeared ahead of us, leading the way. They were bright in the dark. Enchanting.

"They're a trick," Roarke said.

I blinked and shook my head, trying to clear the slight haze in my mind that the lights had created. He was right. As soon as we came to a branch in the path, my dragon sense pulled in the opposite direction of the lights. I turned, heading down the narrow lane with Roarke at my side. Without the guiding lights, it was darker, so I drew my sword and fed it some of my Phantom power. It was a trick I'd worked on, and the blue glow gave us some light to see by. Now that Roarke knew what I was—or at least, part of what I was—so I could use a bit of my strange magic in front of him.

"This maze is clever," I said. "I bet we're going into a more protected area."

The magic felt stronger as we walked, as if we were entering the true heart of Cambridge.

When we finally reached the end, a short path led to the river he'd mentioned. It was wide and slow moving, with buildings on either side. The massive stone structures butted up right to the water, with no room to walk on the bank between the building and the river. To our right, a smaller structure crouched on a stone platform. Long, shallow boats had been pulled onto the narrow strip of shore. It must be a boathouse. Tall poles were stacked against the boathouse wall. For pushing the boat along, perhaps.

I took stock of my dragon sense, unsurprised when it pulled us right.

"We either have to go through the buildings or take a boat down river," I said.

"Boat."

"Yeah."

Together, we put one of the long, shallow boats in the water. They had wide, flat platforms on either side— perfect for standing upon and pushing the boat along with one of the poles. I grabbed one of the tall poles and hopped in. Roarke grabbed another and followed.

I stood on the front platform, while he stepped onto the back. In tandem, we stuck our poles in the water. Mine hit the bottom only a few feet down and I pushed, propelling us forward. We moved quickly down the river, our boat gliding along silently in the dark.

It was a good thing it was so late and this place was full of hard- working scholars. They were all asleep in their beds or had their noses in books, not outside to witness our silent passage.

The thought was still fresh in my mind when a rustling on the shore caught my attention.

I glanced over. A massive, horned demon was running alongside the boat. My heart thundered.

Damn.

A rustling from the other side of the shore caught my attention a moment later. There was another demon, this one spindly and thin. Two more followed behind him.

"We've got company," I said.

"Four more on the right."

I looked over. That made at least eight demons total.

"Where the heck did they come from?" I asked as I pushed us along. For now, the demons weren't jumping in the water to come get us. But they would eventually.

"Maybe they were already here."

Or they had come through the hole in the protection charm Roarke had created. Either way, we had a problem.

I turned to look at Roarke. "Should we each take a bank and get rid of them?"

"We have bigger problems." He pointed ahead.

I spun around. Five other boats were drifting toward us, each manned by a huge Magica. Their power rolled out from them in waves.

"Who the hell are they?" I whispered.

"Security."

"Damn." What the hell were we going to do? I didn't want to fight a bunch of security guards who were just doing their job.

"We're here to see Horatio Penderren," Roarke called. "We mean no harm."

"Then you shouldn't have brought your demon minions." The mage who spoke threw out his hands. A light blasted from him.

Before I could fully process it, a massive net flew through the air and landed on top of Roarke and me, throwing us down. I thrashed, struggling to get up, but the heavy net bound us tight into the hull of the boat. It stung slightly wherever it touched my bare face and hands.

Beside me, Roarke struggled to stand, putting all his strength into tearing through the net. But the thing wouldn't budge. It was like it had wrapped around the bottom of the boat, trapping us inside.

"Don't bother," the guard said. "The Montaris Net won't let you out."

He steered his boat against the stern of ours, the other guards maneuvering their crafts until our little boat was surrounded. I peered up through the net, my skin stinging like mad. It got worse the longer we were trapped under the damned thing.

"We really are just here to talk to Horatio Penderren," I said.

"Then you should have set up an appointment. And mentioned that you were bringing along an army of demons." His face twisted, as if the very idea offended him to his core.

I couldn't blame him if he thought I was here to attack them.

On the shore, more guards appeared to take care of the demons.

"We're not here to do any harm," Roarke said.

"I can hardly trust the word of someone who broke in under the cover of darkness and who possesses the power to compel demons." The guard began to push us along, directing our boat with his.

"We didn't bring the demons!" I cried.

The guard's face turned red with rage. His dark, beady eyes bulged. "Don't lie!"

"I'm not! Just let me talk to someone. Your boss, or anyone. I can explain."

He puffed himself up, raising his reed-thin body to its fullest height as indignation distorted his face. "*I* am the Chief Constable!"

Oooh, shoot. I pissed him off.

"I'm sorry. I didn't bring the demons, I promise."

"Lies!" His venomous gaze met mine as his voice filled with threat. "The Order of the Magica will be very interested to hear about this."

"No!" I struggled to stand, desperate to make him hear reason. He couldn't report me to the Order.

Roarke grabbed my arm, forcing me to meet his gaze.

"Shh!" The noise was short and harsh, but his message clear.

Anything I said would only hurt us. The Chief Constable clearly had it out for us. Me, in fact. Maybe I looked like an ex-girlfriend who had dumped him.

So I shut up, though it was damned hard. I just wanted to scream at the guard that he was a freaking moron. Or turn into a Phantom and drift through this net. But if I did that, I'd have to kill all the guards who saw me in my Phantom form. And I didn't want to do that.

Better to wait and see where they took us, then deal with this once the enchanted net was off.

I lay still, fuming. I could feel the guard's beady gaze on me, seething. I felt his ire like a brand against my skin.

As he pushed us along in the boat, I did my best to keep track of where we were going, noting our location in relation to that of Horatio Penderren. We were heading away, unfortunately.

The river drifted silently below us. Soon, a massive building loomed overhead. Oh fates, the river went under a building. What the hell was in here?

Dim yellow light illuminated the underground river bank. The ceiling was only about eight feet overhead, and either side of the river butted up to a stone walkway. A moment later, the boat was pushed over to the side until it rested against the walkway.

Before I could move, the magic in the net vibrated. It slithered away from the boat, pulling Roarke and me up into the air. One of my lucky necklaces caught on something in the boat and tore off my neck.

"No!" I reached for it, but we were dragged quickly through the air, prisoners in the enchanted net.

I thrashed, trying to escape, but the magic was too strong. The net carried us toward a big door. As if on cue, the door swung open. The net tossed us inside. Roarke and I crashed to the stone ground as the door slammed shut.

CHAPTER FOUR

"What the heck was that?" I scrambled to my feet and raced to the door. I pushed against the wooden surface, but it didn't budge.

The room was small—only about twelve feet by twelve—and the walls and floor were made of massive stone slabs. A single lightbulb hung from the ceiling, shedding a pathetic twenty-five watts on the dingy cell.

I rubbed my arms, my stomach turning. This place felt weird, but vaguely familiar. A bit sickening. I couldn't place it though.

"This damned university has a prison?"

"And some powerful magic." Roarke stood. "I've never seen anything like that net."

"They must have something important they're protecting."

"Or a lot of important somethings. That Constable was not pleased to see us. He *really* doesn't like anyone breaking into his university."

"No." I shivered at the thought of his glee at the idea of alerting the Order. "But this is good, right? We wanted to get away from them so we could sneak away. Now we can."

Roarke could either bust through the wall like I'd seen him do before, or I could walk out of here as a Phantom and hopefully find a key.

"Hopefully." Roarke walked to the walls and inspected them. "Do you want to do this, or shall I?"

"Can you do it quietly?"

"Tearing through walls isn't exactly a quiet business."

"Fair point. I'll try."

I closed my eyes and called upon my Phantom power, waiting for the chilly magic to flow through me.

It didn't.

The usual chill didn't come, nor did my limbs turn a transparent blue. I tried harder, but nothing happened.

"Shit," I said. "Dampening spell."

The best prisons had them. Cass, Nix, and I had been locked up in a place like this when our boss had turned on us. Since then, we'd worked for ourselves. But that prison had felt like this one, with the sickening sense of my magic being repressed. I'd tried to forget the memory, but that was why this place had felt familiar.

"You try," I said.

Roarke just stood there, eventually closing his eyes for concentration. When I didn't feel the swell of his magic, I knew.

"Damn it." I started to pace. We were as helpless as humans in here. "This is no normal university."

"No kidding."

"This was supposed to be a quick in and out—meet a guy, get some help. Who knew universities could be so dangerous?"

Roarke grinned and paced the cell, inspecting the walls again. I did the same to the door, but found only a massively thick slab of wood reinforced by iron straps. There wasn't even a door handle on this side.

This wasn't good.

We needed help.

"Where do you think Draka is?" I asked. "Last week, whenever I needed help, she showed up. But now— nothing."

"Maybe we don't really need the help."

I glanced around at the stone box in which we stood. "I'm pretty sure we do. This dampening spell has made us helpless."

"No, though it is inconvenient."

I paced the cell, my mind racing. I hated being cooped up like this. If only we had our magic. It spurred a memory.

"I once met a Hellhound named Pond Flower." The mental image of the big dog made me smile. "She was immune to charms like this because her power was fueled by hell. So the dampening charm couldn't work on her. We need a bit of that right now."

"If anyone could do it, you could."

"I wish." But the mental image of Pond Flower remained. What I wouldn't give to see her friendly face right now.

Magic shimmered on the air.

"You feel that?" Roarke asked.

"Yeah, it's star—" My jaw dropped open.

A dog suddenly stood in the middle of the cell.

"Pond Flower!" I cried. She was massive—nearly the size of a horse—with brown and white spots and a big smile that allowed her tongue to loll out of her mouth. The scent of brimstone and flame wafted off her.

"Did you just summon her?" Roarke asked.

"Apparently." I approached and scratched her head, then asked her, "So, did you come because I called?"

She just looked up at me, and I got the sense that she was saying, "Yeah, duh."

The last I'd seen Pond Flower, we'd rescued her from living in a dingy castle filled with demons. She'd gone to live in an enchanted forest with the League of FireSouls, which was something like a magical justice league that helped to protect FireSouls from persecution.

"Got any ideas on how to get out of here?" I asked as I scratched her head.

Her brown eyes flamed red, and an eerie black flame burst up from her fur. It didn't burn me, though. Instead, magic rolled out from her, igniting inside me.

"Whoa," I whispered.

The magic pulled on mine, making it come alive inside my chest. It was a bit different than my normal magic. It felt hot, and if I had to guess, I, too, smelled like brimstone.

I closed my eyes and called upon my Phantom form, letting the icy magic flow through my veins. I shivered as it filled me, then opened my eyes to see that my body had turned fully blue and transparent. Pond Flower continued to glow with her black flame. But as I watched, a blue glow extended out from my hand, turning her black flame blue. Soon, she was blue like me, a Phantom dog whose eyes still glowed red.

"That's impressive," Roarke said.

I grinned, then glanced at Pond Flower and removed my hand. The magic inside me died. My body returned to normal. So did Pond Flower.

Shoot.

I touched Pond Flower again, and the magic ignited once more. I shifted to Phantom form. Pond Flower followed.

"I think she's like a conduit. I'm getting power from the Underworld."

"Yeah, you both stink like brimstone."

As I'd thought.

"We'll go through the wall and get you out of here." I knocked on my head for good luck, hoping this would work.

He nodded.

I turned, walking with Pond Flower toward the door, careful not to lose contact with her warm head.

This was so freaking weird.

We walked through the door without any problem, appearing at the darkened riverbank.

A guard to my left gave a strangled shout and stumbled back, his eyes wide.

No doubt he'd never seen the likes of me before. His hand went to his belt where some kind of wand hung from a little holster.

I let go of Pond Flower and drew my sword, turning corporeal and lunging at him. As he drew his wand, I brought the hilt of my sword down upon his head. It cracked against his skull, and his eyes rolled back. He fell like an oak, out cold.

A silvery key ring glinted at his belt.

I knelt and checked his pulse, relieved to feel it beat. Pond Flower stood over his body, staring down at him.

"Thanks, pal," I said to her as I fumbled for the keys. "You can go back and hang out with your buddies in the forest again."

I didn't want her hanging out here where she could get hurt. Better to have her frolicking in the forest.

She licked my hand as I stood, then disappeared. As I turned back to the locked door, I glanced at the water, hoping to see the boat where my lucky necklace had fallen off. The boat was gone.

Damn.

I stepped up to the door where a massive black lock awaited. It wasn't hard to find the matching key. It, too, was massive and black. I shoved it into the lock and twisted until the familiar snicking noise sounded, then pushed open the door.

Roarke stepped out. "That was quick."

"I got lucky." I turned and dropped the keys near the guard, then called on my dragon sense. "We're close. Come on."

We hurried along the stone embankment, sticking close to the wall. A doorway caught my eye, and I pushed it open, revealing a small antechamber. Unlike the grim stone walls that surrounded the river, the walls were paneled with some kind of pretty wood. Glowing sconces provided light. There was a doorway opposite the one we stood in.

"That should lead into the rest of the building," Roarke said.

We slipped inside.

"I think Boadica's College is the one next to this one," I whispered, following my dragon sense.

Roarke nodded and pushed open the door a crack. I dipped under his arm and peered out. A grand foyer stretched in front of us, the ornately tiled floor gleaming in the light of the chandelier above. Weird that the prison was next to such opulence. But then, this whole place was weird.

Two massive doors took up a big part of the adjacent wall. Windows revealed the snowy scene outside. The foyer was dead silent, so we hurried out of the little room and across the tiled floor. Fortunately, the doors weren't locked, and we spilled out onto the massive front steps. An open courtyard stretched in front of us, with buildings looming on all sides.

Frosty air chilled my lungs as I followed my dragon sense down the stairs and to the left.

We kept to the shadows near the building, our footsteps silent. A narrow alley between buildings led us to another courtyard, this one smaller and filed with trees and plants. The sparkling lamps made it look like a fairy land. The buildings here weren't the massive stone ones, but rather like old Tudor houses with the black wood and white plaster.

"That's it." I pointed to the largest building. There were multiple peaked roofs and many tiny, mullioned windows. Roses climbed up the sides, even more beautiful because they were speckled with snow.

We hurried through the garden and let ourselves in through the small wooden door. The foyer was tiny and dark, but warm, with a staircase on the other side.

"I think we go up," I whispered. "Third floor."

Roarke nodded and led the way up the narrow stairs. No matter how light we kept our footsteps, the old stairs creaked. At the third landing, warm yellow light glowed.

As soon as I reached the top, I caught sight of a room to the left of the stairs. Bookshelves crammed full of leather-bound tomes covered every inch of the walls. A fire glowed in the hearth. It smelled of books and woodsmoke, and the heat bowling out of the room warmed my icy skin.

In the middle of the room, a man leaned against the desk, his arms crossed over his chest as he watched us.

Horatio Penderren.

"Roarke Fallon." Horatio nodded at Roarke. "I didn't expect to see you again."

Roarke stepped into the room. "I suppose not. But I need your assistance."

"You trust me to provide it?"

Trust? What had happened between these two? It was impossible not to catch a serious undercurrent on the air. There was history between these two guys, and I definitely believed Roarke when he said that he and Horatio weren't friends.

"You're our only hope," Roarke said.

Oh, I didn't like the sound of that. I wanted more than one hope. I wanted multiple hopes.

"I'm Delphine Bellator." I stepped into Horatio's line of sight.

His green gaze snapped to me. He was slender, about forty years old with a scholar's face. Spectacles perched on his nose, giving him a slightly owlish air.

Horatio gestured to two chairs in front of his desk. We sat while he went behind his desk and took the massive leather chair that looked like it had seen a lot of butts.

"How can I help you?" Horatio asked.

"I have power that I can't control. But it's a weird one. Can I rely on you not to share what you hear from me?"

He nodded, his gaze serious. I searched his face, looking for any sign of perfidy, then glanced at Roarke, who nodded. Roarke didn't necessarily like the guy, but he trusted him. That was a good enough endorsement for me.

Horatio nodded and listened intently as I explained how I attracted demons with my new Ubilaz power. And that I had also taken an ice demon's gift.

"But the thing I don't get," I said, "is how I can control the ice power but not the demon attraction. And I once had the power of teleportation—I was very good with that."

Horatio leaned back in his chair, his gaze thoughtful. "The control of magic is a complex subject, but there are a few general principles. It is easier for you to control powers you were born with. Were you born with the teleportation gift?"

"I think so, yes." And I was actually a Phantom, so it made sense I could control that.

"As for powers that you obtain from other sources—it's easy for you to control lower category powers. Ice is a Cat 2. The Cat 5 power will be almost impossible to control."

"So, for example, bringing back the past—what about that?"

Horatio nodded. "A rare power, that. Not normally associated with a category of demon. I've never heard of anyone mastering it."

That made me feel a bit better.

"Do you have that gift?" he asked.

I shook my head. "Just trying to understand."

The power had shown up out of the blue, but I hadn't taken it from a demon. Which meant it was my own, and eventually I'd have better control of it.

From the crease of his brow, I could tell that he didn't believe my lie, but I wasn't going to tell this guy everything about me. Keeping things close to the vest was too ingrained.

"We're here to see if you can help Del control the demon attraction," Roarke said. "She needs to learn to repress it."

"I can try."

"How do you do that, exactly?" I asked.

"My gift is manipulation of the part of your brain that helps you control their magic. I can help you focus and direct your energy toward that. Hopefully, it will work." He glanced at Roarke. "It doesn't always, however."

I glanced at Roarke, whose expression was stony.

Holy undercurrent, Batman. There was something here.

I'd bet big money that Roarke hadn't needed help controlling his own power—he was the epitome of self-control. But someone else close to him, perhaps?

Now clearly wasn't the time to ask.

I turned back to Horatio. "Can we do it now?"

He nodded and stood, then came around the desk to kneel by my chair.

"I'm going to touch your shoulder." His voice was soothing, like a doctor's. "Your brain may feel….tingly for a moment. That's just me figuring out exactly what we're dealing with."

I couldn't help but stiffen when he touched my shoulder. Slowly, I sucked in a breath, waiting.

Horatio stumbled back, his eyes wide.

"What's wrong?" Roarke demanded.

"Did it work?" I asked.

"I didn't have a chance." His gaze traveled between the two of us as he stood. "You have a block in your mind."

"A block?"

"Yes. A rare spell. Someone—or something—has cursed you."

Confusion ricocheted through me. "What the hell do you mean?"

"I don't know how or when, but you have a rare obstruction in your mind that limits your control of your powers. It's not just that higher category powers are harder to control—you have something in your mind that is making it nearly impossible to control certain gifts."

Shit. "Why? How?"

"A seer prophesied that someone like you would come to me for help," Horatio said. "It was fated."

Roarke made a noise low in his throat, the kind that indicated what he thought of fate. Many supernaturals didn't believe in it—which I thought was totally nuts. Magic was real, so why not fate? I *definitely* believed. There were all kinds of ways to figure out fate—seers, prophecies, spells.

"I find that hard to believe," Roarke said. "You just stumbled into a seer who predicted Del's arrival here?"

Horatio straightened. "We have some of the most advanced seers in the world here, over in Cassandra's College. I make a point to visit them every year."

"That's a bit often." I might believe fate, but I didn't want to know too much about it. Knowing what was coming could be stressful. But some supernaturals liked to know. They were the magical equivalent of those humans who called the psychic hotline. Except in this case, it was true.

"I know." He grinned sheepishly. "But I like to stay on top of things. And it helps with my work. Like with you. About five years ago, Cassandra, our oldest seer, prophesied that a woman would come to me needing help. But that it would be beyond my capability. She requested that I bring you to her."

Hope and confusion fluttered in my chest, two butterflies duking it out for superiority. Cassandra might have answers—to problems I only now realized existed?

At least it explained my miserable control over my magic.

"Can we go see her now?"

Horatio nodded. "She doesn't work as late as me, but she'll want to see you."

Roarke and I stood, and Horatio led us down the stairs to the foyer. Near the door, cloaks and hats hung from the wall. He grabbed two heavy black cloaks and two hats and handed them to us.

"Wear these," he said. "You didn't have an appointment, so I assume you broke in. We don't want the Chief Constable to find you."

I smiled weakly and said, "Yeah, that would be bad."

Roarke and I put on the cloaks and hats. Mine was just about the right length, but Roarke's was far too short.

"Hopefully no one will look too closely," Horatio said. "You're much larger than any of the other professors."

"Is that what we're dressed as?" I asked.

"Yes." Horatio tugged on his cloak and hat, then hurried out into the snowy night.

Roarke and I snuck out behind him, and we moved quickly across the campus, keeping to the shadows. We saw no one as we passed by old buildings and beautiful courtyards.

"Nearly there." Horatio led us around a silent pond.

A massive stone building sat on the other side. We skirted the pond and went around the side of the building. When we reached a small wooden door, Horatio pulled a keyring from his cloak and undid the lock, then ushered us into a small, dark hallway.

Horatio squeezed around in front of us. "Keep your footsteps silent and follow me."

We followed him down the hall, then up a back staircase to the fourth floor. He knocked on a door at the end, and we waited for at least five minutes. It felt like ages.

Finally, a young woman opened the door. She was beautiful, with long dark hair and sleepy eyes.

"Cassandra," Horatio said.

This was Cassandra, the oldest seer? She looked to be only twenty. Subtly, I tried to feel out her magic, sniffing the air and breathing deeply. I got a hint of something ancient—more of a feeling than a scent or taste or sound like some signatures. She was older than she looked.

"Horatio? What are you doing here at this hour?" her voice was raspy with sleep.

He pointed at me. "This is the woman you prophesied. The one with the block on her magic."

Cassandra's green eyes widened. "Really. Well, come in. Come in."

She stepped back and gestured us inside. We followed Horatio into the almost painfully modern space. Everything was chrome and leather and looked slightly out of place against the old stone walls of the building.

"Take a seat." She led us to two long leather couches that faced each other across a coffee table. She and Horatio took one, Roarke and I the other.

I sat in the hard seat and leaned toward her. "What do you know about me?"

She shifted closer. "Not much. But you have a rare spell that has been placed upon your mind. Something old that I've never seen before. It makes it difficult for you to control your magic."

"Who put it there?" I hated that I couldn't remember my past.

"I don't know," she said. "But I do know you are important. And that the spell is harmful."

"No kidding. I've been a magical mess lately, unable to control my powers. Sometimes I can, sometimes I can't."

"Yes. The block affects particular gifts. You are able to control some gifts but not others, am I correct?" she asked.

"Yes. Horatio said that my own powers are easier to control, along with lower category powers. Ice and things like that."

She nodded. "That would make sense. Those are easiest for any supernatural to manage, so you can control them despite the block. And some of your powers are new?"

"Um…" I didn't want to confirm or explain how I got them. Obtaining new powers was strictly forbidden since normally you had to steal them from other supernaturals if you wanted to get them. Since that was exactly how I'd gotten most of my powers, I didn't want to share. Though the Phantom power had appeared without me having to steal it, it was a particularly dangerous power and one that no one needed to know about except those I trusted.

She sat back. "Don't worry. I don't need to know."

"Why? You trust me?" I asked.

"Enough," she said. "I've seen that you have a role to play in something important and that I must aid you. I can't help you get your magical control back, but I have something that might help."

She stood and went to the corner of the room. She touched the wall, which shimmered and disappeared to reveal a massive black safe. When she opened it, a messy trove of books and boxes threatened to spoil out. After a moment of digging, she pulled a leather folder out and returned to us.

She held it out. "This is for you."

I took it. "What is it?"

"A map. With directions. It will lead you to answers. I found it in the back of our main library. I think it's been there for centuries. When I touched it, I had the vision of you. It's how I knew you would come to Horatio."

Hope unfurled in my chest as I opened it. The leather was brittle under my fingertips. Carefully, I laid it open on my lap.

Squiggles and lines, along with a *really* foreign language, met my gaze. It made Cyrillic or Arabic look easy to understand, and I spoke neither of those languages.

Disappointment welled. "It's indecipherable."

"You're supposed to be able to read it," she said. "I'm certain of it."

"Well, I can't."

She frowned. "I wonder if it's part of the block on your power."

Damn it.

A horrendous rattling ring rent the air. I jumped, seeking the noise. On a silver end table, a sleek black phone rang.

Cassandra's face paled, and she hurried to it, pulling it off the hook and holding it up to her ear. I could just make out the babble of a voice on the other end as Cassandra's gaze traveled to meet mine.

She hung up with a clatter. "You've got to go. That was the campus-wide warning system. The Chief Constable is looking for two fugitives who brought a demon army onto the campus. Apparently they escaped from the dungeons. I imagine that is you."

I jumped to my feet, the leather folder clutched tightly in my hand. "It is."

"You need to be quick," Horatio said. "He'll turn you over to the Order of the Magica in a heartbeat. They don't know you're here yet, but they'll find you. We could cover for you, but if he finds you, we can't protect you."

"Is there a graveyard or a haunted place nearby?" Roarke asked, his voice tight.

"A small pet cemetery behind the building," Cassandra said. "In the rose garden."

"It'll do."

"Is there anything else you can tell us?" I begged.

Cassandra nodded to the map. "That is all. It will help you find the answers you seek."

But I couldn't read it! Though there was no time to worry.

Horatio surged to his feet. "I'll lead you out."

"Thank you, Cassandra." I turned and followed Roarke and Horatio, clattering down the dark, narrow staircase.

At the main landing, we turned away from the front door and made our way to the back of the building. A narrow kitchen led out to the back garden where the scent of roses drew us to the pet cemetery. It was lovely, with benches and a fountain. Glittering white snow fell lightly upon it all.

"There." Horatio pointed.

"Thank you," I said.

He disappeared back into the building.

"Here." Roarke held out his hand for me.

I gripped it just as I heard a rustle in the bushes. "Hurry!" I hissed, my heart racing.

Roarke held out his free hand, palm out. Magic flowed from him, the scent of sandalwood and the taste of wine strong. Then he drew back his fist and slammed it forward. A burst of light exploded as it stopped dead, like he had punched a wall.

Roarke wrapped his arm tighter around me and tugged me forward, stepping into the glow. I glanced behind us, catching sight of the Chief Constable's enraged face just as the Underpath swept us up. We hurtled through space as gravity disappeared. I tightened my grip on Roarke.

A moment later, we stepped out into the woods near Roarke's house. He dropped my hand immediately. It was pitch black, and I could barely make out the trees, though I could hear the river rushing nearby.

"Here?" I asked.

"My house is protected from demons. And I didn't want to draw them to your place." He pulled on my hand, and we hurried through the forest.

We raced up the stairs to the porch, dashed through the front door, and slammed it behind us. Only once we were inside did I realize that Roarke was still holding my hand.

A shiver ran up my arm as I looked up at him. Adrenaline from our escape still raced through my veins. His, too, from the brightness of his eyes. His gaze riveted to my face, warming with a heat that made my heart pound

Oh, man, he was so hot.

His hand tightened on mine, and he pulled me closer. I stumbled forward, my chest bumping into his. Warmth flowed through me, and my skin lit up with electricity. I tilted my head up to his, giving him my best *I want you* look.

This was it. He was going to kiss me.

The heat in his beautiful eyes made it clear. The way they traced over my lips. His own full lips parted just slightly, enough to make me want a taste more than my next breath.

He dipped his head just slightly, sending my heart rate into the stratosphere. The warmth of him almost burned me as he stepped closer. My skin prickled with awareness.

He hesitated, so long that I stopped breathing. So long that I decided to take matters into my own hands and prove that I wasn't being paranoid about his recent distance.

I stood on my tiptoes, almost having to jump because he was so tall, and pressed my lips to his. It was more of a brush, really, because he immediately pulled his head away and stepped back, letting go of my hand. A wall slammed down behind his eyes.

His expression went completely blank.

What?!

It was suddenly much colder without his touch. Embarrassment was hot oil poured on my head. I wanted to sink into the floor and live there under the house, a weird hermit person.

"We need to figure out what it says on that map," he said.

"Uh… Yeah."

That was the best I could come up with in this circumstance.

"I have a friend that I can send a picture of the map to," he said. "He or she may be able to read it."

"Thanks." My mind buzzed with embarrassment and confusion. "I'll, uh, text a picture to Dr. Garriso. Maybe he'll know something."

Roarke turned on the lights as I laid the map out on the narrow table by the door. We each took a turn snapping a photo with our phones, then sent them to our friends. My skin tingled the whole time, like even *it* was embarrassed, wanted to run off my body, and get away from what an idiot I was.

"It may take a while to hear back," Roarke said. "But as long as we're in the house, we're fine. It's protected from demons."

Desperately, I tried to make conversation and act like this was normal. I could call him out on his mixed signals, but then I'd have to acknowledge my ridiculousness, and this just seemed easier.

So I said, "I guess they'd have good reason to want to take you out. There'd be one less person trying to keep them in hell."

"Exactly, though they don't often try. I do like to sleep without worry."

Sleep. Wow, that sounded great. It'd been a while since I'd had a nap. Or a shower. I could smell myself.

"I'm going to get a shower while we wait to hear back about the map, okay?" I said.

"Sure. I'll put something on to eat."

Well, that made it hard to stay annoyed with him. "Thanks."

I hurried up the wide wooden stairs to the bedroom I'd used last time I was here. It was as ski lodge chic as ever, with beautiful rustic furniture and a massive fireplace. I stopped by one of the wide windows and peered out, looking for demons. The river glittered in the moonlight below, but there were no demons that I could see.

Didn't mean they weren't there—or that they wouldn't show up. Having them stalk my every move, drawn to me like freaking flies to honey, was hell on my nerves. With the Order of the Magica also possibly on my tail, this was turning out to be a pretty rough week.

I touched my fingertips to the comms charm at my neck, igniting the magic. "Cass? Nix?"

"Hey!" Cass said.

"Are you safe?" Nix asked.

"Yeah."

"What do you know?" Cass asked.

"Not much." I told them about Cassandra and my powers.

"Oh, that's such shit." Cass frowned. "I'm sorry."

"Thanks."

"But they couldn't help you get rid of the magical block on your mind? Or control your power?" Nix asked.

"No. But they gave me a map that's in a foreign language. It's supposed to lead me to answers. We're waiting to hear back from Dr. Garriso or Roarke's friend. Hopefully one of them can read it."

"That's a start," Cass said. "Let us know how it goes."

"I will."

"How's Roarke?" Nix asked. "Everything good there?"

My face heated. "Yeah. About that. I did something stupid."

"What?" they demanded in unison.

"I tried to kiss him."

"Aaaaand?" Cass said.

"It went…badly. He pulled away immediately." My mind replayed the way it had all started. "But it was weird! I mean, he clearly wanted to kiss me. He was giving me the most obvious look, and he grabbed my hand and pulled me toward him until our chests touched, and he even leaned down!"

"Hmmm." Nix's voice was thoughtful. "He would have definitely had to lean down. That's the only way you'd have managed to reach his lips, he's so damned tall. So he was definitely interested."

"Exactly!" A memory poked at me, sending hot embarrassment flooding through my veins. "But I did kinda have to give a little hop to get up to him though."

"Oh man," Cass groaned. "Once you have to jump to reach a guy…"

"Yeah." I grimaced. *This* was the exact reason that setting up permanent residency under the house seemed like a great idea. Except it was Roarke's house, which would turn me into a weird, troll-like stalker. "It wasn't a big jump though."

"He has to have a reason," Cass said.

"That's what I'm afraid of." I leaned against the wall, thudding my head against it.

"You could just ask him," Cass suggested.

"I'd rather shave my eyebrows off than admit to what just happened."

"Yeah, give her some time to recover from the humiliation," Nix said. "And remember… He's the Warden, and she's technically still a fugitive from his hell. And don't forget what Dr. Garriso said about him turning his brother in to the Order."

Nix's words only fueled my fear. "Exactly. He says he's on my side, but it's so hard to trust that. I thought I was crazy suspecting him, but this proves I wasn't. I'm not saying he has to kiss me to prove he's on my side—that'd be pretty freaking creepy of me—but he's giving me such mixed signals. He *clearly* wants me. I may have had to jump, but the pre-jump moments were *very* clear. But something's holding him back. And he talked to me way more last week than he's talking to me this week. He doesn't trust me."

"Do you trust him?" Cass asked.

"Not really." I had a hard time believing anyone other than my *deirfiúr* were on my side. It'd taken me years to grow to trust Connor and Claire.

"It's smart to be wary," Nix said. "Between running from the Monster from our past and keeping our FireSoul natures a secret, wariness has kept us alive. And Roarke—he's got so much power. One change of heart, one word to the wrong person...."

I'd be done. Was that why he'd cooled off in his approach to me? Because he still wasn't sure of me? He could just toss me aside any time.

The idea of being abandoned felt all too familiar. Like I expected it.

Nah, that was nuts. I had no reason to think that.

"Yeah, be careful. But not so careful that it hurts you in the end," Cass said. "Give Roarke a chance. There's gotta be a reason he's changed his tune."

My thoughts exactly. But I was afraid of what that reason was.

CHAPTER FIVE

After hanging up with Cass and Nix, I showered quickly, then dressed in my old clothes. I could try borrowing some from Roarke, but that was now out of the question. It'd just feel weird to wear his clothes after my failed jumping-kiss. Too personal.

I headed down the stairs to the kitchen, my heart thundering. I tried to distract myself by studying how beautiful Roarke's home was, but it didn't work very well.

As I'd expected, he was in the kitchen, pulling something out of the oven.

"Vegetarian lasagna." He set it on the counter and glanced at me, his gaze so normal that it made me wonder if anything had happened at all.

"Thanks. That was quick."

"I had it in the fridge." He gestured to the box of wine on the counter. "Help yourself."

He'd gotten my favorite kind. "You got that for me?"

"I asked my housekeeper to pick it up."

So, he didn't want to kiss me, but he'd obtained my favorite wine. What the heck?

I poured myself a mug, desperately pretending everything was normal and that I hadn't just made an idiot of myself. "Want one?"

"Sure."

I poured him one as he set two plates on the table.

"Dr. Garriso hasn't texted back." I set my phone next to my plate where I could hear it if he sent a message. "Did you hear anything from your guy?"

"Not yet."

"Damn." I dug into the lasagna, burning my mouth in my haste.

"Careful."

Good advice. I didn't follow it, chowing down instead. Not because I was hungry, but because I *really* didn't want to make conversation.

After I'd taken my last bite, both of our phones buzzed at the same time. We grabbed them. I pulled up the message, my heart sinking when I read Dr. Garriso's response.

"He doesn't recognize it," I said. "At all."

"Florence did." Roarke met my gaze. His was dark. Full of questions. "But she can't read it."

"What language is it?" It was a long shot, but maybe there was a Google translate or something.

"It's a dead demon language. She doesn't know which."

"What?" I dropped my pone onto the table. "I'm supposed to know an ancient demon language?"

84

"Apparently."

Damn. "That's not good."

"It's strange, that's certain. Are you sure you don't know anything about your past?"

"Nothing." I rubbed my forehead. "What are we going to do? How do we read it if everyone who knows the language is dead?"

As soon as the words were out of my mouth, I knew. *Dead.*

Death couldn't stop me.

"I think you know what to do," Roarke said. He was on the same page.

"Yeah. But can I? What about the block on my mind that Cassandra mentioned?"

"That gift is an inherent one, so you can still get around it. If you try hard enough."

He was right. The experiment with the *A.J. Goddard* hadn't gone well. But I *had* brought it back.

And the person who had written this map had a message for me. If only I could talk with them. Even if we didn't speak the same language, it was better than nothing. We could figure it out.

"I can try," I said.

"Do you want to try now?"

I nodded, then pushed back from the table. "In the living room. There's more space."

I grabbed the map from where it sat on the counter and led the way into the mini ski lodge that Roarke called a living room. He'd built a fire while I was in the shower, and it crackled away merrily in the stone hearth.

Comfortable couches and a massive coffee table were crouched in front of it.

I set the map on the coffee table and took a seat in front of it. Roarke took the chair to my left. It all looked so normal, with the exception of the fact that I was about to bring back the dead.

The squiggles on the map stared up at me, daunting.

I could do this. The shipwreck had been practice, and I'd succeeded there. Kinda. Whatever block was over my magic, I could get around it sometimes. Cassandra said I might be getting stronger.

So I'd have to try to be strong.

With that in mind, I rubbed my remaining lucky necklace for luck and then knocked on my head for good measure.

I closed my eyes and drew a deep breath, focusing on the hum of magic within me. When the voice of Horatio Penderren echoed in my head, telling me that no one had ever truly mastered this gift before, I pushed it aside. This was harder than anything I'd ever tried before, since I wasn't technically in the place where the map had been created.

Since the visualization trick had worked last time, I tried it again. My magic formed as a dim orb of light in my mind. I reached for it, straining. After a moment, my fingertips itched as if they were close. I tried to picture what the scene had looked like when this scroll had first been created. Some supernatural had sat down and left me a message.

The image grew in my mind, stronger and brighter. Magic hummed in the air. The space around the map shimmered slightly, as if something were trying to come forward.

My heart raced with the effort, and sweat broke out on my skin. My magic still felt wild, uncontrollable, but I was directing it in the right way.

Something *was* happening. The air was definitely shimmering.

Then a wall slammed down in my mind, crushing the orb of light that had symbolized my magic. The air around the map stopped shimmering. My magic died on the air, leaving it still and dead.

I collapsed back on the couch, panting and exhausted.

The cozy fire-lit scene was just as normal as it had been before I'd started, much to my dismay. Tears prickled at my eyes. Embarrassed, I blinked them back, determined not to cave, and looked at Roarke.

The sympathy on his face just made my eyes prickle worse. I wouldn't let the tears escape, though. They stayed stuck in my eyeballs, right where they belonged.

"It's not easy," Roarke said.

"No." Thankfully, my voice was firm. "But it's necessary. What kind of Guardian am I if I can't do what's necessary?"

This magic would kill me eventually. I wouldn't even have a chance to figure out what it meant to be Guardian. Without any control, demons would find me. One day, in such great numbers that I couldn't protect myself. Maybe I'd bring others down with me. More than likely, I would.

"You can do it, Del. We just need to find a way."

"Yeah, yeah."

"I'm serious. Just because you failed now, doesn't mean you will always fail. Sometimes we try our best at the most important thing we will ever do, and still we fail."

My gaze snapped to him. There was first-hand knowledge in his voice. "What do you mean? What did you fail at?"

He shifted, his gaze suddenly blank.

"Does it have anything to do with your brother? Is that who Horatio tried to help you with?" I couldn't help but poke, wanting to know now more than ever. *Needing* to know.

Roarke frowned. "This is the second time you've asked that."

"And the second time you haven't answered."

"I told you not to pry. Not everything is your business."

But it was. If he'd really turned his brother in, it was pretty freaking relevant.

"I really can't talk about it." Roarke's voice was heavy.

"No, you won't."

"Maybe. But that doesn't change the fact that I want you to succeed. And that I understand the failures that can be had on the path to success." His gaze was sincere. He *meant* what he was saying. He couldn't be that good at faking it. "You can do this, Del."

I sighed. Odds were strong that he was a good guy, right? I'd thought so countless times.

But he'd turned his brother in to the Order, that dark little voice inside of me said.

Shut up, you.

I had bigger problems than worrying about Roarke. True, he knew my secret and could turn me in. But I just had to trust him for now and fight my own stupid instincts to blow things up that seemed too good to be true. Because I was currently facing a seemingly insurmountable problem.

All I could do was focus on that and try.

The dream came in fits and starts, feeling so real that I knew it had happened before.

I stood in the middle of a circular room. Windows covered the walls, allowing a view of mountains rolling into the distance. The tower was an older part of the castle, the place where I spent most of my time.

Alone.

The sword I gripped in my hand hung limply, pointed toward the ground. Blisters stung my fingers and palms, right where the hilt of the sword rubbed. The blade was small, like me, a child's practice weapon.

Hopelessness welled inside of me. No matter how hard I tried to learn, still I failed.

I was clumsy and inept, capable of only the most rudimentary moves.

How did a girl like me, child of such a powerful family, do so poorly with a skill I needed to learn?

"Try again."

I jumped at the sound of my teacher's harsh voice, gripping my sword tight and blinking back tears. I sniffed, trying to stay quiet, and resumed my stance.

"Wrong!"

I jumped again, unable to help myself. No matter how much I expected to hear the censure, it stung every time. With a deep breath, I focused on the move to come. If I didn't master this, my parents wouldn't permit me an audience with them. Showing them what I'd learned was the only opportunity I had to see them.

"Again!"

I resumed my stance, then lunged forward, sweeping out with my sword. Before the movement was even over, I knew that I'd done it improperly.

The door slammed shut behind me, even worse than the sound of my teacher shouting.

He'd left.

The key clicked in the lock.

My shoulders drooped and I sobbed.

I was worthless. No way I could do this.

A sweep of blue light caught my eye, rushing in through the open window.

Draka.

The Phantom dragon landed gracefully beside me and enveloped me in her wings. Comfort and warmth flowed through me. Not as good as the rare moments when my mother embraced me, but good enough.

As good as I was going to get.

I woke with a gasp, my chest feeling empty and heavy at the same time. Darkness blinded me. I blinked frantically until my vision adjusted. Pale moonlight filtered through the windows, illuminating the artistically rustic furnishings in the lavish bedroom.

Roarke's house.

I was in Roarke's house. I was an adult. No longer the child in my dreams.

I pushed a shaky hand through my hair, which was damp with sweat, and sucked in calming breaths of cool air.

Had that been me in my dream? Sure felt like it. I'd never had a dream of my childhood before.

So was that why I'd always been so good with a sword? I'd been practicing since I was a child? I hadn't been very good back then, though. It had been something that my parents had wanted me to accomplish, but I couldn't.

My heart ached as yearning for my parents swept through me. It didn't matter that my memories hadn't been particularly good. I still wanted to see them, desperately. I'd lost some of that desire over the years as I'd grown to love Cass and Nix, my new family. But this felt just like when I'd been fifteen and awoken with no memory. I longed for my family. Wished for them.

Tears prickled at the backs of my eyes, but I forced them away.

There was no time to be weak or wallow in self-pity.

So what if my parents had locked me in some horrible tower and made me practice with a sword until I had blisters on my hands? And that now, I still wanted to see them more than anything?

Focusing on that wouldn't fix the problem ahead of me.

Had they even loved me? asked the mean little voice inside my head.

Draka had loved me, though. I tried to focus on that. But I hadn't seen the Phantom dragon since she'd appeared to me last week when she'd helped me kill the Ubilaz demon. Was she okay?

Fates, I hoped so, even if I didn't get to see her again.

At least I had one figure from my past on my side. And my *deirfiúr.* Roarke and I had agreed to go to Ancient Magic in the morning and present our problem to Cass and Nix. Hopefully they'd have some ideas. Between all of us, we'd come up with something.

Right?

CHAPTER SIX

The wind was bitter cold when Roarke and I stepped out onto his front porch the next morning on our way to Ancient Magic. Sunlight sparkled through the trees, and the rush of the river cut through the silence of the morning.

I glanced around at the forest, but saw nothing besides the big trees that surrounded Roarke's place. We hurried down the steps to the drive where his car was parked about ten yards away. Dreams of the car's ferocious heater were warming me from the inside when the snapping of a branch made my hair stand on end.

I whirled around, expecting a bear.

Instead, I saw a demon.

Stupid me, expecting a bear. I knew what hunted me, and it wasn't bears.

The demon was a tall, slender variety that would look harmless if not for the fact that it had six-inch claws that dripped with a neon yellow substance.

Poison. No question.

Its yellow gaze searched mine, as if trying to decide why I didn't look like an Ubilaz demon but possessed its power. Finally, it hissed, "Abomination!"

"I'm getting *so* sick of that word." I sneered at him. "What, you don't like me?"

At least, they *really* didn't like the idea that I'd taken another demon's power.

"Get to the car," Roarke said. "I'll take care of it. You can't risk killing it and adopting another power."

As much as it annoyed me, he was right. Until I knew exactly what this demon's power was, I didn't want to steal it. I sure as heck didn't want to become poisonous.

I backed toward the car, keeping my gaze trained on the demon. I was so intent that I almost didn't notice the other monsters who crept from the woods.

All demons. Two dozen of them. No, more than that.

"Roarke!"

"I see them."

The demons must have congregated during the night, hiding behind trees and waiting for us to exit. I adopted my Phantom form, letting the icy magic flow through me.

A tornado of black mist whirled around Roarke, and his magic surged on the air. A moment later, he burst off the ground, his dark gray wings carrying him into the sky. He was grace and power incarnate. He could handle this.

But more demons slunk from the trees.

More, more, more.

So many different species, so many different types of magic. The signatures were intense—everything from the smell of rotting eggs to the feel of slime, slipping between my toes.

Roarke swept through the air, picking up demons and hurling them into trees so hard that their bodies broke like matchsticks. He was so fast that he was nearly a gray blur, streaking through the air. Their claws never had a chance to land. Screams rent the air as he worked, demon bodies piling up left and right.

But no matter how fast he killed them, more appeared, creeping toward us from the trees. It was a nightmare.

My palms began to sweat, and my muscles ached to take action.

Watching Roarke fight the demons alone was *torture*. Just standing here, waiting to be rescued, was the worst. I should be helping. *I* was the one who'd caused this problem.

Soon, there were three demons only twelve feet away. Roarke was taking care of the rest, but he was outnumbered. There were just *too many*. While he was breaking the neck of one massive demon, four others jumped upon his back.

No!

I searched his attackers frantically for poison claws but saw none, thank magic. But they were still overpowering him.

We needed help. Where was Draka?

"Draka! Pond Flower!" I cried.

But neither dragon nor dog showed.

Roarke held his own against the four—no six, now—demons who had piled onto him, but there were still too many dropping down from perches in the trees.

I couldn't just stand here. If saving Roarke—and myself—meant stealing some powers, so be it.

And maybe I wouldn't steal powers if I killed remotely.

I raced to the car and shoved the folder with the map underneath the windshield wiper, making sure it was held down firmly.

Though my hands itched to draw my sword, I ignored it, calling instead upon the ice magic that I had stolen from the other demon. I let the magic chill my fingertips as it built inside me. When I felt like I was at max capacity—filled with icicles from my toes to my head—I threw out my hand and imagined shooting a massive icicle at the demon nearest me.

A shining spear of ice hurtled through the air, skewering the demon through the chest. My heart lodged in my throat as I watched to see if his soul would fly out of his body and cling to me like the others had.

Instead, he fell like a sack of rocks.

Fates alive, I could slay demons remotely without taking their power!

I grinned, then turned to another demon. The big, pale beast was only five feet from me and coming fast. The sword that he gripped in his hands was about four times bigger than mine, a comically large piece of steel that I was sure he knew how to use.

I called upon the ice power, throwing it at him before it had a chance to develop fully. The icicle that hurtled toward him was far smaller than the last one I'd thrown. It pierced him through the chest, but he didn't fall. His sword arm lowered and he stumbled, but kept coming.

Shit!

I leapt out of the way, reaching for my ice magic once more. Apparently, if I wanted a nice big icicle, I had to let it charge fully inside of me, like a battery powering up. The magic swelled in my chest as the demon raced toward me me. When I felt like my skin was bursting with icy cold, I threw my hands out toward him.

The icicle that shot from my palms was massive, plowing straight through his chest and out the other side. The demon that stood about ten feet behind him was struck as well. He fell, impaled by the icy spear.

Jackpot! Two for one.

I spun to find more prey, grateful to see that Roarke had killed three of his demon attackers and was finishing the last three. Bodies littered the leaf-strewn ground around us, all slowly disappearing and returning to their Underworld.

In relatively quick succession, I killed eight more demons. I had found a clever way to buy myself the time to wind up my power. Jumping and dodging only worked for so long. Avoiding weapon blows and blasts of fire magic took a toll on a girl.

"Line them up like you're playing pool," Roarke shouted.

I grinned, remembering my two for one from earlier. There were two demons about twenty feet away. If I moved just a bit...

I sprinted to the left, letting my magic charge as I ran. When the demons were lined up, one after the other, I sent a massive bolt of ice at them. It was bigger this time and flew with a speed that made a bullet look slow.

It punched through the first demon and straight through the second, lodging in a tree behind them.

I was getting good at this!

It didn't take long to finish off the rest of the demons. By the time we were done, the forest around his house looked like a war zone in hell, demons of all species scattered around.

Quick as a flash, Roarke shifted, leaving behind his half naked, dark gray demon self and masquerading as a normal guy in jeans and a black jacket.

I wasn't sure which I liked better, to be honest.

"Hurry," he said. "There's no telling when more will show up. I think our proximity to the portal made it easier for them to sense you."

The reminder made the glow of victory fade and my stomach pitch. He was right. The demons would keep coming, over and over. Even though I could now kill them, I didn't *want* to spend the rest of my life fighting demons the moment I stepped out of my house. And if they showed up at the wrong moment, they could kill innocent people or those I loved in order to get to me.

I hurried to the car, taking the map off the windshield, and climbed in.

Roarke took off, driving like it was the Indy 500.

"It's getting worse," he said. "More demons every time."

"Yeah."

"Think your sisters will have any ideas?"

"I hope so." I played with the twin lucky pendant around my neck, regretting the loss of the other. "We've managed everything before this."

For good measure, I knocked on my head.

"Anything this bad?"

I thought back to the last few months, during which Cass, Nix, and I had come face to face with the Monster from our past. "Yeah."

He glanced at me. "No wonder you're tough."

"Honestly earned."

We reached the factory district in no time flat, and Roarke found a spot right in front of my green door.

"I need to change and get a bag from my place," I said. And if I was being honest, I wanted to get another lucky pendant. Probably switch this current one for another, since things hadn't gone so great while I'd worn it.

Roarke followed me up the stairs to my place.

"Stay here." I pointed to the living room, then darted into the bedroom.

It didn't take me long to dig out a small bag. I was about to duck into my trove to get a different lucky pendant when a knock sounded at my apartment door.

"Del!" Cass hollered at the top of her lungs.

I heard Roarke open the door for her and knew she'd bust into the bedroom any second. Now was not the time to let myself in to my trove. And if I was being truly, totally honest with myself, the lucky charms were a crutch. I was clinging to them because I had no control over anything else in my life.

I spun and hurried out into the living room.

Cass stood in the middle of the room, wearing her usual fitted, brown leather jacket and jeans. "Well? Any luck with Dr. Garriso?"

"No. Where's Nix and Aidan?"

"Aidan's got some work to take care of. Nix is at P & P, getting coffee before she starts at Ancient Magic."

"Let's go. I need to talk to her." I headed to the door, then pulled up short. "Damn it, I shouldn't go to P & P. I need to be in a place blocked from demons. And I don't want to draw them to the cafe."

Fates, this sucked.

"Ancient Magic fits the bill." Cass glanced at her watch. "Nix should be back there any minute. Let's meet her down there."

"Great." I met Roarke's gaze.

He nodded, then led the way down the stairs to the street outside. When I reached the door, I hesitated, peering out.

Looked normal. No demons in the park or hiding behind cars. It was only a matter of time though.

I darted out and turned left, slipping inside Ancient Magic behind Cass. Roarke followed. The place looked so normal, cluttered with artifacts and rich with the signatures of various spells. While I felt...not normal. Not even close.

The door opened behind us and I spun.

Nix stepped in, her cheeks bright from the cold and a paper cup clutched in her hand. "How's it going?" she asked. "Any answers?"

"Nope. Dr. Garriso knows nothing, and Roarke's friend says that the map is in a dead demon language that I'm supposed to be able to read."

Nix's eyes widened. I didn't have to look at Cass to know that hers did the same.

"Dead demon languages are a problem," Cass said.

"And you're supposed to be able to speak it?" Nix said.

Movement outside on the street caught my eye. It took a second to recognize the dark-haired man hurrying toward our door, but when I did, my breath caught.

It was Orson Reyes, the Order guy who gave Claire her assignments. She appeared in the window a second later, hurrying behind him. I could just make out what she was saying through the glass.

"You're mistaken! There's no way she's involved."

My heart plummeted to my feet just as the Order member yanked open the door and burst into the shop. Claire hurried in behind him.

"Which one of you is responsible for the demon attack on Cambridge University?" His beady dark gaze darted between Nix, Cass, and me.

We all stared at him, dumbfounded.

"Don't play dumb. I am Orson Reyes, representative of the Order of the Magica. I have it on good authority—from the Chief Constable of Cambridge— that someone living at this address has a demon following and that they attacked the university."

"What are you talking about?" Roarke demanded. "Those are serious accusations."

Orson held up my lucky pendant. The one I'd lost on the campus.

Shit.

"The Chief Constable apprehended an intruder who wore this. A Tracking Mage on their staff identified this address as the home of this object. It is my responsibility to find the person."

Bad freaking luck.

His gaze zeroed in on me, on the matching pendant that I wore around my neck. "It was you."

He stalked forward, his eyes widening as he neared. "Your magic… It's…"

He sniffed the air and licked his lips, as if he were trying to get a feel for my magical signature. His magic filled the air, bringing with it the sound of rustling leaves and the scent of chalk.

Oh, shit. He was using his Sensor Mage powers. I stepped back, not wanting him to pick up on my demon powers.

"Stop!" He held out a hand, but I kept backing up until I hit the wall. "You're the one with the Ubilaz powers! You're responsible for the surge in demonic activity. I can feel it. The powers aren't in an object at all. They're in *you!*"

I opened my mouth to dispute the claim when a demon appeared on the street outside of the shop. His burnished red skin indicated that he was probably a fire demon.

Oh, eff this.

Could the timing be worse?

I glanced at Roarke, whose gaze was trained on the demon. His expression turned predatory.

"I have no idea what you're talking about," I said, moving left, hoping that the Order member's gaze would follow me and give Roarke time to slip outside and get rid of the demon before anyone noticed it.

Orson's gaze did follow me, but it snapped back to Roarke as soon as he moved for the door. As if the demon had called his name, Orson turned to look onto the street.

He pointed and said, "Then how do you explain that?"

"Just a random demon? You really should do a better job keeping track of them," Nix said.

Roarke strode outside and made quick work of the demon, dodging its initial blast of fire magic and then lunging and breaking its neck.

"No." Orson shook his head and pointed at me. "It is her. I can feel it. Claire was supposed to address this, but she has failed to do so. Because she is friends with the culprit."

"It's not her!" Claire said.

"Of course it is." Orson sneered.

Quietly, Roarke slipped back into the shop.

How the heck were we going to get out of this one?

"She's a mercenary," Cass said. "She wears a charm to attract demons so that she can more easily get the bounties. That's all it is."

"Yeah," Claire said. "I've been really jealous of that charm. She racks up twice the kills that I do."

"No." Orson's voice was hard as a rock. "That's bullshit. She's the one we seek. I can feel her."

Damn.

From behind the man, Roarke's gaze hardened. He reached to the small table at his side and picked up a heavy clay jug. Quick as a snake, he brought it down on Orson's head. The vase shattered, the magic it had once contained drifting up toward the ceiling as pale smoke, and the man collapsed.

Roarke crouched and pressed two fingers to Orson's neck. "Out cold."

"We can't kill him!" Claire cried. "He's my boss!"

"If I wanted to kill him, he'd be dead." Roarke stood. "But we need time to figure out how to fix this."

I sat heavily on an old chair pressed against the wall. "This is bad."

The Order of the Magica knew who I was. What could I do?

"Very bad." Cass rubbed her forehead.

"We have to make him forget what he knows," Roarke said.

"How?" I asked.

Roarke turned to Claire. "Does your brother have a potion that would do it?"

"No. Not something like this."

Nix stepped forward. "Aerdeca and Mordaca might be able to manage it."

"With blood magic?" I asked.

It was one of their talents, but they normally just sold charms out of their shop, Apothecary's Jungle, because blood magic was so dangerous. And on the edge of the law. I didn't know if I wanted to dabble in that.

Roarke frowned. From his expression, he *definitely* didn't want to dabble in that.

"They'd use blood magic to influence his memory?" Cass asked. "But that's the mind. It's the most dangerous thing to try to manipulate."

"And it's illegal," Roarke said.

Nix held up her finger. "Only if it's without consent."

Roarke frowned at Orson's prone body. "I don't think he's going to consent."

Cass stepped forward, her expression hard. "Look, I know you've got a thing for the rules and all, but Del doesn't stand a chance if the Order knows what she can do. At best, they'll toss her in prison. Worst—she's dead."

"And that's the more likely scenario." Nix shot me an apologetic glance. "Sorry. It's true."

"Yeah, I know." Still made me sick to think of it, though.

"So, what's it going to be, Roarke?" Cass asked. "You going to stick to your rules and throw Del under the bus?"

"No." Roarke's voice was firm. He didn't even hesitate, which made me feel a bit better. "We can go to these women and ask if they can help."

"Good," Nix said.

"How do you know about this anyway?" I asked. Nix wasn't particularly good friends with Aerdeca and Mordaca—that was more Cass's territory.

Nix shrugged, her gaze sad. "When Cass remembered her past, and you remembered your true last name, I wanted to know more about my past as well."

My heart hurt for her. For me, too. We knew almost nothing of our lives before we woke in the dungeon owned by the Monster from our past. My only memory was of being a slave to a man who wanted to control FireSouls. And my dream last night hadn't revealed anything good.

"Did you have any luck?" I asked.

"No." Disappointment was stark in Nix's voice. "Memory is a hard one for them—particularly remembering. And recalling big pieces of the past isn't possible. The process would kill me. I decided it wasn't worth it."

"But they can make Orson forget?" Cass asked.

"I hope so," Nix said. "It's at least a possibility."

"Then let's try," Roarke said. He still clearly didn't like the idea of relying on illegal magic, but he'd do it. For me.

Why, I didn't know. But I had to thank the fates that he was on my side.

CHAPTER SEVEN

Getting Orson's body into the car wasn't fun—again, I felt like I was in the mob—nor was the surprise attack by another demon who appeared out of nowhere right after we shoved Orson into the backseat. Claire took care of the demon as I climbed into the passenger seat. Cass and Nix piled into the back with Orson, who slumped against the window.

"We really need to get this demon thing taken care of," Cass said as she watched Claire kick some demon ass.

"No kidding." It was for sure getting worse. I clutched the bag I'd brought, which contained the map.

Fortunately, we made it to Darklane without further incident. The neighborhood where Aerdeca and Mordaca lived and ran their shop looked dark and dingy even in the light of the mid-day sun. No matter how brightly it shined, it couldn't cut through the grime covering the once colorful paint of the old buildings.

Roarke found a spot right in front of their door, but we didn't have to be particularly stealthy with a body in this neighborhood. No one would dream of going to the police here. Particularly to help an Order member.

Roarke slung Orson's body over his shoulder, his face slightly pained, probably at the idea that he was currently carrying an Order member into a place that practiced black magic. But when his gaze slid over me, it cleared. Like he was reminded of why he was doing this.

I turned to the stairs, trying to reconcile the distant guy he'd been lately with the one who was here now, protecting me by breaking his own rules. I failed.

Before I reached the top, the door opened.

Aerdeca, dressed in her usual impeccably tailored white pantsuit, stood in the doorway and stared at us with a blond brow arched.

"You're alive, Del." Her voice was cool as rainwater, but sweeter. Her lips twitched up at the corners, just a couple millimeters. It was the biggest smile I'd ever seen her give, but it was genuine.

She and her sister had been at the battle that had killed me. I'd hoped they hadn't seen my body and that we could play it off as a bad injury that'd taken a while to recover from. No luck, apparently.

"Wasn't ever dead," I said.

"Hmmm." She blinked her blue eyes impassively. "Then to what do I owe this pleasure?"

Her magic flowed over me, sounding like chirping songbirds. With her pale good looks and lovely voice, you'd think she was a pushover. Far from it. I'd seen her in action. She was tough *and* scary.

Two things I respected.

"Can we step inside?" Roarke asked.

She sighed and stepped back. "I suppose."

We hurried into the dimly lit foyer that felt like it should be in the Addams family movie. All dark wood walls with black and white tile flooring. Ever-blooming black roses climbed up the staircase bannister.

Aerdeca gestured with white-tipped nails and headed to the back of the foyer. "You'd better bring him this way."

We followed her across the tiled floor and into a short hallway that led immediately into a workshop. Shelves stuffed full of crystals and jars lined the walls. A hearth lay dead in the corner, its embers now dark. The scent of wood smoke lingered, along with a floral aroma from the herbs that hung from the ceiling. A massive wooden table sat in the middle of the room.

Aerdeca walked around to the other side of the table, looking entirely out of place in her white suit. She should be in a boardroom instead of here.

She pointed to the table, blue eyes calm. "You may as well put him on the table."

Roarke offloaded his burden, still knocked out cold. Cass and Nix leaned over him, peering down at his slack face.

"What is it that you want?" Aerdeca asked.

"I'd like you to make him forget something," I said.

Her brows rose. "That's not easy. It'll be expensive."

"It's worth it." Ancient Magic had been doing well lately, bringing in more money than we were used to. I'd have less cash in my account and lucky charms stash, but paying the bill wouldn't be a problem.

"Excellent," Aerdeca said. "Let me get Mordaca. She's going to need to help."

"Oh, boy." Cass whistled as Aerdeca left. "Mordaca's not going to like that. This is like midnight for her."

I grinned. There was something so prickly about Mordaca that I kind of liked poking at her.

It didn't take long for Aerdeca to return with Mordaca trailing behind her. Mordaca's hair was up in its usual bouffant, though slightly flattened on one side. The mask of black eye makeup that she wore was smudged, and her black silk robe draped over her Barbie-doll figure. Even in the middle of the night—which it was, for her--she looked like a sexy lady of darkness who'd just gotten off an all-night bender.

"Do you even realize what time it is?" Mordaca's raspy voice filled the room, followed by the whiskey taste of her magic. "It's the middle of the night."

"It's two in the afternoon," I said.

"It's the middle of *my* night." She pointed at herself with one of her glossy black fingernails, her brows arched. "And that's what matters."

I grinned. "Sorry about that. We were hoping you'd be willing to help us."

"For a price."

"Aerdeca mentioned that," I said. "It's fine."

"Memory eraser for this fellow." Aerdeca poked him and glanced at me. "He's an Order member, isn't he?"

"And I assume he knows something incriminating about one of you three." Mordaca's gaze traveled between me, Cass, and Nix.

"Me!" I stepped forward. Mordaca knew we all possessed forbidden magic, but I didn't want her pointing it out in front of Roarke. "I'm the one."

"Ah, that little trick you pulled with coming back from the dead?" Aerdeca asked.

I frowned.

"Don't worry," Mordaca said. "Your secret's safe with us."

"And soon, this fellow won't have it either." Aerdeca pointed to Orson. "But memory control is difficult. Very precise. You'll have better luck if he forgets a certain period of time rather than a thing."

"That's fine," I said. "Can we do the last few days?" Ever since he'd learned what I was. We could knock this problem out real quick.

Aerdeca shook her head. "Not if you want him to have any kind of higher functioning reasoning left. The best we can do is half a day. He'd be groggy and feel a bit weird, probably have a killer headache."

That wasn't ideal.

"Could you give us a moment?" Roarke asked.

Aerdeca and Mordaca gave identical shrugs, then left the room.

Roarke turned to us, keeping his voice low. "That should do it. He'd forget what the Constable told him. Once Del has mastered her magic, Claire can tell him that she's fixed everything and hopefully this problem will disappear."

"How, though?" I asked.

"He mentioned that he thought the demon magic was imbued in an artifact. She can give him a dummy artifact and say that she got rid of the spell that was causing the demons to flock to it."

"That would work," Cass said.

"What about the Constable?" Nix asked. "He might know stuff."

"It sounded like he just thought she was causing trouble and now he's reported it to the proper authorities. And without Del's lost necklace, he'll have no proof."

"That's good," Nix said. "Could work."

"Yeah, I think it will." I looked toward the door. "Mordaca? Aerdeca? You can come back now."

They entered the room. Mordaca rubbed her hands together "Let's get to work."

"So, you want the maximum memory loss that will still keep his mind intact?" Aerdeca asked. "That's about half a day."

"Yes."

"Excellent." Mordaca sauntered to a shelf and removed a heavy onyx bowl and silver-bladed knife.

Aerdeca drifted to Orson's side and picked up one of his hands.

A shiver raced over my skin and guilt prickled. A hand clasped mine, warm and familiar. I glanced over at Cass.

"This is the right thing," she said. "Not just because I don't want anything bad to happen to you—which duh, I don't—but you're the Guardian."

"Whatever that means," I muttered, but my heart warmed at her words.

"Something important," Roarke said. "And you won't learn what it is with the Order after you."

I nodded, forcing myself to watch Aerdeca take the knife from Mordaca and make a slender cut at Orson's wrist. As she drained the blood into the bowl, I asked, "This is a lot like those old doctors who bled their patients, isn't it?"

Mordaca nodded. "It's a bit barbaric, but effective."

"For our magic, that is," Aerdeca said. "It didn't work so well for the doctors."

Mordaca sneered. "A bunch of monkeys, mimicking something they didn't understand."

"Doctors had been copying blood sorceresses, only without the magic?" Nix asked.

Aerdeca nodded. "Yes. One of them probably saw a blood sorceress heal someone once and tried to achieve the same effect. Didn't work, obviously, but that didn't stop them."

Yet another reason humans shouldn't be allowed to mimic magic.

After a few more moments of letting Orson's blood drain into the bowl, Aerdeca returned his wrist to the table. Mordaca dabbed a gray paste onto the wound as Aerdeca gathered ingredients from the shelves.

They worked in tandem, quickly and efficiently, never bumping into each other. It was a dance that they had choreographed to perfection. Aerdeca poured the powders and liquids into the bowl of blood, while

Mordaca stirred with a paintbrush. When it began to sizzle, they both smiled.

In low voices, they began to chant over the bowl. The language was foreign, but the intent was clear. Memory loss.

Finally, they quieted, then took the bowl to Orson. Mordaca raised the paintbrush, which dripped grotesquely with blood, and painted a line on Orson's forehead. It smoked and sizzled, then disappeared, sinking into his skin.

She stepped back and smiled. "That should do it. He'll wake in a few hours, confused, but fine."

"Thank you," Roarke said.

"Don't thank us, pay us," Mordaca said.

"We will." I stepped forward. "But first, I was wondering. A seer said that a magical block was placed upon my ability to control my powers. Can you remove that?"

Aerdeca frowned and stepped forward. She raised her dagger, holding its point toward me. "Prick your finger on this. I will try to see if we can help."

I poked the blade's tip with my index finger until pain flared. A drop of blood welled around the silver tip and I removed my hand.

"I'm going to touch your head now." Aerdeca raised a hand and I nodded.

She placed her fingertips against my forehead as she licked my blood off the tip of her blade. Her magic pulsed on the air, the sound of chirping birds and the feel of a breeze. My mind fuzzed briefly, my thoughts going blurry.

Aerdeca's eyes widened and she stepped back. "No, we cannot remove that. It is far too powerful, and far too dark."

My heart dropped. Too dark for the woman who licked blood off a dagger? I wanted nothing to do with that. "Then if you can make Orson forget, can you help me remember something?"

"Maybe," Aerdeca said.

Mordaca frowned. "That's a far more difficult and dangerous matter."

"I'm not afraid of danger." My whole life was danger these days.

"How dangerous?" Roarke asked.

"It's nothing like making that man forget a few hours. This goes deep into the mind. Depending on how old the memory is, and how deeply it's in her mind, it can be deadly," Mordaca said.

"What do you want to remember?" Aerdeca asked.

A lot of things. "How much can I remember?"

"Pick one thing, start there," Mordaca said. "You may not even manage that."

Shit. "I'm supposed to be able to read an ancient demon language. I need it so that I can interpret a map that has directions on it. But I don't remember how."

"Did you ever know how?" Mordaca asked.

"Yes. According to a seer called Cassandra."

"Cassandra?" Aerdeca looked at Mordaca, whose dark brows had risen comically high. "The one at Cambridge?"

"Yes."

"She's a descendent of *the* Cassandra," Aerdeca said. "The one from Greek myth. If she said it, then it's correct. She is never wrong."

"Good. Let's do it."

"How long ago did you forget the language?" Mordaca asked.

"No idea."

"You don't even know *when* you once knew this language?" Mordaca exchanged glances with her sister, then looked back at me. "This could kill you."

"You'd be surprised," I said. "I seem to be good at popping back."

Aerdeca grinned. "True."

And either way, this wasn't as risky as having dozens of demons coming at me out of nowhere. This procedure only risked my life. The demons were a threat to anyone who was around me.

"Do you have this map with you?" Mordaca asked. "That will help us."

"I do." I pulled it out of the bag I'd brought.

"Right, then." Mordaca pointed at Orson's body. "Someone needs to get him out of here, then we can start."

Roarke picked up the body and glanced at us. "Where do I take him?"

"Back to Claire," Cass said. "She'll know where to deliver him."

Roarke looked at me. "Be careful. I'll be back."

I nodded, then swallowed hard. Just because I'd come back from death once, didn't mean I was keen to repeat the experience. But this was the only way.

Roarke left, Orson draped over his shoulder, and I turned to the blood sorceresses. "I don't need to get on the table, do I?"

"Depends on how much blood we have to take," Aerdeca said.

"Is blood loss what would kill me?"

"That, and the shock of the magic, if it has to go too deep into your memory."

"Great."

"We'll start with you sitting in a chair," Aerdeca said.

Oh fates. I was going to let the blood sorceresses poke at my mind. I was used to the supernatural, but this was a bit creepy even for me.

Mordaca went to the chair near the fire and pulled it over to the table. She set it up as if someone were about to sit in it and have dinner. Mordaca pointed to it. "Sit here. Put the map on the table."

"Thanks."

Mordaca and Aerdeca hustled around the room as I sat in the chair and put the map on the table. I positioned it so that I could read it.

Cass and Nix came to stand next to me.

"You'll be fine," Cass aid.

"Yeah, a little dying never killed you."

I grinned. "True."

Mordaca appeared at my side and nudged Cass out of the way. Nix followed, setting up vigil on the other side of the table with Cass. Mordaca set two large bowls on the table, one near each wrist.

My heart raced. "Could this turn my mind to mush, you poking around and all?"

"It's a possibility," Mordaca said. "But we'll be careful. Honestly, death is more likely with this, if you have a hard time locating your memory of the language."

Great.

Aerdeca appeared at my other side, two glinting silver blades in her hand. She passed one over to Mordaca.

"Raise your wrists," Aerdeca said.

"Both?"

"This spell requires more blood. Enough to make you woozy and weaken your mind's defenses."

Barbaric. I grimaced and raised both hands, swallowing hard.

Mordaca and Aerdeca each took one of my wrists. Pain flared when the knives sliced through my skin.

"It will help if you try to focus on what you want to remember," Aerdeca said.

"Okay." I did my best, imagining being able to speak whatever language was written on the parchment in front of my face.

The scent of my blood drifted toward me, making my stomach turn. I did my best not to look, but the drip, drip, drip of the dark red stuff was hard to ignore.

"Isn't that enough?" Cass asked.

"Do you feel woozy, Del? Tired?" Aerdeca asked.

I shook my head, trying to see. "No."

"More it is, then," Mordaca said.

The blood continued to drip, filling the bowl until a sheen from the light overhead developed on the surface. Tiredness dragged at me.

"I think I feel it," I said.

"Good." Aerdeca put my hand on the table. Mordaca followed. From the corners of my eyes, I could see them sprinkling herbs into the blood. They stirred the concoction with their daggers, then laid the blades on the table and picked up boxes of matches. I was having a hard time keeping up with what they were doing.

"Eyes on the paper." Aerdeca pointed to it. "The real fun is about to start."

I glued my vision to the map, noting that the words were starting to wiggle in front of my face. I blinked, trying to make them stay still.

The sound of matches striking filled the air. Unable to help myself, I peeked up just in time to see Aerdeca drop her match into the blood. It burst into flames, sending up a thick black smoke that smelled sweet and rich and horrible.

I coughed, gagging slightly, as Mordaca and Aerdeca pushed the bowls closer to me so that I breathed in more smoke.

No wonder people had a shitty opinion of blood magic. This was gross.

"We're going to touch your head," Aerdeca said.

"Uh huh." My voice slurred, and I realized that I was still bleeding from my wrists. That wasn't good, right?

Two hands lightly touched my hair and I swayed.

"She doesn't look good," Nix whispered.

"She's still bleeding," Cass said.

"Shut up," Mordaca snapped.

"Hey!" Cass stepped forward.

"Guys, is cool," I slurred, squinting at the lines in front of my face. What the hell had I gotten myself into?

Magic suddenly pulsed on the air, strong and rich. Mordaca's tasted like whiskey, making my throat burn. Aerdeca's chirping birds got louder, as did the feeling of a breeze over my skin.

But even weirder was the feeling in my head, as if thin tendrils of smoke were unfurling in my mind, poking around all the crevices in my brain. It felt like it originated in my mouth.

Oh, ew. Was that why they'd lit my blood on fire? I shoved away the thought, not wanting to focus on what exactly was going on here.

"Focus on the words in front of you," Mordaca said. "We're going to try to find the memory."

The blood smoke choked me and hazed my vision and I squinted at the squiggles. Minutes or hours passed as my mind drifted. It was like being drunk on magic and blood loss. My vision began to darken at the edges.

"Anything yet?" Mordaca asked.

My head bobbed, dipping down toward the table. The words still looked like gibberish.

"Nooo," I slurred.

"Try harder," Mordaca said.

I blinked and squinted, my head bobbing again, almost hitting the table. The words danced in front of my eyes. For a second, it looked like one said *west*, but then it just looked like a squiggle.

"You... almost had it," I said.

The room began to spin around me as my vision narrowed in on the words in front of me. My breath heaved in and out of my lungs, loud as a jet plane in my foggy head.

Aerdeca's whisper drifted through the fog in my mind. "She's fading. We should stop."

"No!" I thought I screamed, but it came out only as a whisper.

"Too dangerous," Mordaca said. "You're losing too much blood. This could kill you."

"No, one more… try." I blinked, trying to gather every ounce of will that I had. But my head bobbed toward the table again and the words blurred in front of my eyes.

"You're dying, Del."

Dying. The word spurred an idea and I said, "I don't… die."

I called upon my Phantom magic. It took a few tries, but I caught the shivery thread of my gift. Ice slithered through my veins, but it carried clarity to my mind. I glanced at my arm, grateful to notice that I hadn't fully transformed. I was only slightly blue, hopefully little enough that it could be explained by blood loss.

I blinked, using the last of my Phantom-given strength to focus on the words in front of me. Just as they began to swirl and form something recognizable, I lost the thread of my magic.

Then passed out cold, the pain of my head thunking on the table the last thing I knew.

The dream pulled me back in time, away from the blood sorceresses' lair and into that same tower in the mountains. It was dark this time, with only a sliver of moon visible through one of the arched windows.

Draka, in her human form, stood on the other side of the room. She was as beautiful as ever, pale and blue and transparent, her face as ageless as the moon appeared to be.

"It's not very far." She pointed to the ground in front of her. "You can do it. Just teleport to here."

I stared forlornly at the spot from the other side of the room, my stomach screaming with hunger. I wouldn't be fed dinner until I could teleport at least a few feet and I couldn't remember the last time I'd eaten.

It was my mother and father's new plan for getting me to learn my magic. Just like with my swordplay, I was terrible at my magic.

Tears prickled at my eyes and I squeezed them shut hard. I was *not* a crybaby.

If Draka hadn't come to help me, I'd be all alone up here. I needed to be grateful for that. She was the best friend I'd had in all my eight years.

"I'm trying," I said.

"You must try harder. *Believe* in yourself."

But it was so hard, when I'd failed so many times before.

I squeezed my eyes closed and focused on my magic, pretending that it was a glowing pink light. When I caught it in my hand, I envisioned the spot where Draka stood and gave it everything I had.

The ether sucked me in. When I felt my feet on solid ground once more, I opened my eyes.

I was only halfway across the room! The tears spilled over. "I'll never learn!"

Draka hurried close, wrapping her arms around me. "Yes, you will. You must practice. It is harder for you."

"Because of the curse?" I sniffled against her ghostly shoulder, feeling warmed by her embrace.

"Yes, dear. Because of the curse. It is a dark spell that makes your magic harder to control. But you must fight it. Practice, practice. You will learn."

"But if I am cursed, does that mean that I am bad?"

"No. No, of course not. But you must make sure to always do what is right. That will guide you. Do what is right. Prove you are worthy and the magic will come."

"If I do what is right, will my parents love me?"

"I do not know. That isn't something you can control. They are heartless and do not understand you. They do not know how. But you are their heir and must fulfill a role. Therefor you must learn."

It didn't make me feel much better. Draka loved me, but she was a Phantom dragon. She didn't understand feelings the way people did.

But she did love me. Unlike my parents.

"Couldn't I just tell my parents why I'm bad at my magic?"

"You must not." Draka leaned back and looked at me. "They would not believe you or think that you were telling tales."

"I could tell them that you told me."

"They must not know I exist, or they would drive me away."

She was right. In my heart, I knew that Draka was my biggest champion—the one who protected me. She came to me when I needed her. But my parents feared the Phantom dragons. Most of our people did.

I stepped back. "Why have I been cursed?"

"I do not know, but I suspect it is because someone does not want you to accomplish something. A dark shadow stalks you. You must learn your magic, because the shadow cannot get whatever it wants. That would be disaster."

Determination fired in my chest, pushing out the hunger. Whoever it was, they weren't going to get their way. Because I would learn my magic. I *would*.

CHAPTER EIGHT

I woke with the taste of dust in my mouth and the dream at the back of my mind. Just like last time, my chest ached with longing. I wanted to see my parents so badly that it was a physical pain, like a sword blow to the chest.

I sucked in a hard breath and tried to banish the thoughts.

The room was dark, but the smell familiar.

Home? I blinked in the dark and sat up, my head spinning.

"Whoa, careful." Roarke's voice came from the darkness. The bedside light flipped on. He was sitting in a chair near the bed, his hair mussed as if he'd been sleeping. He leaned close, propping his arm on the mattress as his gaze searched mine.

"What happened?" I asked.

"You passed out at the Apothecary's Jungle." Anger laced his voice. "When I returned, they'd taken so much blood that you'd almost died."

"They said that might happen." Memories flowed back in fits and starts. I'd remembered the language, right? I thought so.

"Well, it was dangerous."

"I'm fine, though." Except that my mouth tasted like a feather duster and I felt about three thousand years old. I shifted on the bed, my arm brushing Roarke's.

He pulled away immediately. He coughed, then said, "Good. I'm glad you're feeling better."

"Have you been sitting here this whole time?"

"Ever since I brought you back."

What the heck? And yet he was being so distant. There were questions I wanted to ask, but more than that, I wanted to know if the procedure worked. I didn't feel any different.

"How did it go with Orson?" I asked. "Did he get back to his place with no memory?"

"I delivered him to Claire. From there, we drove him back to his house in his car and left him in the driveway. That was about sixteen hours ago. I've had surveillance on him since then. He woke, was confused, but hasn't spoken to anyone about you. I think it worked. We'll have to keep an eye on him though."

Relief made my chest feel light. "Thank you."

"You just have to learn to control the magic. Because if the demons keep coming for you, he'll sense a problem again. He found you once, and he'll be able to do it twice."

"Yeah. I know. Where are Cass and Nix?"

"In the living room, playing Scrabble."

"Oh shit."

As if on cue, I heard the sounds of an argument.

"That is *not* a word!" Nix cried.

"Is too! Ferbacious means particularly ornery!"

I grinned at Roarke. "Scrabble is a dangerous game in our family."

"I can see."

I struggled to sit fully upright, my muscles aching and weak. My hair felt like it was three weeks dirty, and I was pretty sure I smelled like some kind of forest animal. A glance at the clock showed that it was 2:00 a.m.

"I'm going to shower real quick, then we'll give this map a try."

Roarke stood, dragging a hand through his hair. "I'll go supervise the Scrabble."

By the time I made it out to the living room, Nix had won and was doing some kind of victory dance. She looked a bit like a chicken, but it worked on her. I could hear Roarke in the kitchen, poking around.

"He's making coffee," Cass said.

"Awesome." I staggered to the couch and sat.

"How do you feel?" Cass asked.

"Spectacular."

"Liar."

I shrugged. "Fake it till ya make it, right?"

Cass frowned. "Not sure that applies in this instance."

"I can make it work." The leather folder was perched on the coffee table, as if it had been put there just for me.

It probably had.

I sucked in a deep breath and picked it up, then opened it.

The squiggles on the lines were still squiggles. I squinted at them, trying to make sense of what I was seeing. Slowly, they coalesced to form words. Not moving on the paper, but in my mind.

"It's working?" Nix asked.

"Really?" Cass leaned close.

"Yeah. It looks familiar." I tilted the map slightly. "It's in Wales, I think. North Wales. There are directions for getting somewhere, but they're really confusing."

"Nothing's ever easy," Cass said.

"No kidding." I studied the map and words. "There's riddles. It looks like we need to get there, then figure it out as we go."

"But no idea what's on the other end, huh?" Nix asked.

"No."

"That's proper quest material right there," Cass said.

No kidding. Only I wasn't sure if I really had the energy for a quest. I sat back and looked at my friends, grateful to be in my own place for a little while with the people I loved. Things had been crazy lately. Too crazy.

"I might have had a dream about my past," I said. "A couple dreams."

"Yeah?" Cass asked.

"What happened?" Nix asked.

I told them about being a little girl and practicing with the sword and the magic. About how my parents hadn't wanted me, but Draka had helped me.

"Oh man, I'm sorry." Sympathy gleamed in Cass's eyes. "That sucks."

"Yeah," Nix added. "I'm jealous you're both getting your memories back, but it sucks big time that you aren't getting good memories."

The embrace of the Phantom dragon tugged at my memory. "Yeah, but I have Draka. Whatever she is. Wherever she is."

"She's some kind of Guardian, huh?" Nix asked.

"Yeah. Like a dragon nanny." My childhood had been *weird*.

"Maybe the map will take you to her," Cass said.

"I doubt it. She's come to me three times. Why would I go to her now if she can just come to me?"

"Good point," Nix said. "Do you know why you were in a tower in your dream? Or where it was?"

"No. But if the dreams are true, which they must be since Draka is real, then I've had this block on my magic since I was a kid." And I'd used the visualization trick whenever I wanted to control my magic since then. "Draka also mentioned that a dark shadow stalked me."

Nix frowned. "Oh, that's not good."

"It put the curse on me." I frowned, wishing I knew what the hell was trapped in my mind. So many memories with answers, all out of reach.

Roarke stepped out of the kitchen, two coffee cups in hand. "Coffee?"

"Yes." Del, Nix, and I spoke in unison.

Roarke handed coffee around, got a couple more from the kitchen, then sat on the couch next to me, careful to keep distance between us.

"How's it going with the map?" he asked.

I bent over it, pointing. "We have to go to that place. It's called Cwm Y Ddraig. It's a little town, I think."

"Let's Google it." Cass pulled out her phone and tapped something in. After a moment, she grinned and held the phone up. "Found it!"

"That was easy," Roarke said.

"That was just the first part." I nudged the map across the table so that he could see a bit better. "All those little squiggles are words. They're clues, but they're totally obscure. Things like *finding the Black Mountain* and *journeying the Lake-So-Deep.*"

He frowned and leaned back. "Then we need to figure it out when we get there?"

"So you're coming with?" I asked, shooting my *deirfiúr* a look that said *get lost.* I didn't know if it was the blood loss or what, but I was ready to have it out with Roarke. I shoved the embarrassment of my jumping kiss to the back of my mind and met his gaze.

Cass and Nix stood silently and drifted out the door.

"What do you mean, am I coming with?" Roarke asked. "Of course I am. I'm here to help you until you figure out what you are."

Annoyance surged and I stood, stalking around the coffee table. "Because it's your job?"

"Yes. And because I want to help you."

"Because you like me? Then why haven't you spoken to me almost at all in the last few days? Why haven't you kissed me again when you *clearly* want to?"

He was at my side in a heartbeat, gripping my arm firmly but gently and yanking me to him. "You want me to kiss you?"

When he put me on the spot like that, I didn't know what to say to him. Yeah, I did. But I couldn't fess up to it after I'd tried and failed to kiss him before.

So I went for the gut instead. "I don't know what to make of you. I don't know if I can trust you."

His brow creased, annoyance on his face. "Seriously? After I broke my most important rule to keep you out of the Underworld, you can't trust me?"

It was on the tip of my tongue to tell him I'd spent a lifetime not trusting people, but then he'd ask why. And I'd have to explain being a FireSoul and hiding my true identity from everyone but my *deirfiúr*.

Instead, I said, "You're pretty freaking secretive."

There was stuff beneath his calm demeanor. He was like Lake Laberge, all calm on the surface with stuff underneath. Was there a shipwreck in his past?

"Because I won't discuss my brother?" he asked.

"I've heard you turned him over to the Order. You can see how this would be a big deal to me, right? Because *I* don't want to be turned in to the Order. And if you could do it to your brother, you could do it with me."

"You know nothing." He pulled me closer, until I could feel the heat of his body.

My heart raced, galloping away with all my good sense.

Up close, I could see the pain in his gaze.

"You want me to kiss you?" His voice roughened.

I stared at him stupidly, unable to speak. I was mad, but I was also stupid. So yes, damn it. I did want him to kiss me. He took my silence as a yes and swooped his head down, crushing his mouth to mine. My head swam, and my skin heated.

Roarke's arms enveloped me from behind, pulling me so close that I could feel every inch of him as his lips expertly moved upon mine. They were soft and firm at the same time, so skilled that I shivered, imagining I felt his kiss everywhere. My heartbeat thundered in my ears as his hands, strong and sure, traced my back.

When he finally pulled away, I thought I saw stars. I blinked to bring his face into focus.

"You have secrets, too, Del." His gaze was serious. "You need to trust me if I'm going to trust you. I have my reasons for the last few days, but I'm not keen on sharing until you do a little bit of that yourself. And you're sitting on a mountain of secrets."

He was right. *So* right.

And I didn't like it.

I pulled away and turned toward my bedroom, giving him my back. "I need to speak to Cass and Nix. I'll be back."

I stalked to the exit and pulled open the door. Nix and Cass stumbled down the stairs, just out of sight. I scowled at the dirty eavesdroppers and pointed my finger down the stairs.

Chagrined, they turned and hurried down, and I followed. We ducked into the first door, which was Nix's place.

"So, how much did you hear?" I demanded as the door shut behind us.

"All of it," Cass said.

I shook my head. "You guys have no shame."

Nix nodded. "None."

"So how was the kiss?" Cass wiggled her eyebrows.

"None of your business, is what it was."

Cass nudged Nix with her elbow. "Oh, that means it was good."

"Yeah," Nix said. "For sure. But what did he mean about secrets?"

"I don't know!" But I totally did. "I've told him everything but…"

"The fact that we're FireSouls, right?" Cass asked.

"Because you didn't want to put us at risk," Nix added.

"Yeah." I paced the small apartment. "But he knows everything else."

Cass sighed. "Being a FireSoul is a pretty big deal, dude. It's who we are. It's shaped our whole lives. So I can see how that one secret is actually many secrets."

"Yeah," Nix added. "It's the reason we met in the Monster's prison. We've built our whole business on it. We run our lives around it. It's the reason none of us trust worth a damn and have two friends besides each other."

"I mean, we live fairly weird lives," Cass said. "Roarke's bound to have noticed and wondered why."

133

"Well, he lives a pretty weird life himself," I said.

"Which is why you should maybe consider fessing up to him," Nix said. "Laying it all out there."

Shocked, I whirled to look at her. "You trust him with that kind of information? *You?*"

Cass's brows had jumped up almost to her hairline. "I can see me making that suggestion, but you, Nix?"

"Yeah." She nodded decisively. "I know I've been suspicious of him, but I've been watching him and thinking about it. After the thing with that asshole Orson and how he took care of business and stayed by your side, I'm cool with him. If he was ever going to turn you in, it would have been when that jerk walked in here blathering his accusations."

"*True* accusations," I said.

"Exactly. And all of it leads back to Roarke. He's got a stake in this. If the Order of the Magica finds out he's protecting you, he's in just as much trouble as you are. But he looked an Order member in the face, then hit him over the head and massively broke rules that we know make him uncomfortable. For you. I see no benefit for him in any kind of long con. If he wanted to turn you in, he'd have done it by now. So I think you've got to trust him. Tell him the whole lot."

Stunned, I stared at her. "But then you guys are at risk, too."

Nix shrugged. "We're always at risk. And ever since Cass hooked up with Aidan and told him the whole, dirty truth, our lives have been better."

She was right. But Aidan was so clearly trustworthy.

Or was I only thinking that in hindsight because I'd watched him with Cass for the last few months? He'd protected her, helped her, loved her.

Didn't I want something like that?

Whoa, Nelly. The cart was really getting ahead of the horse here. Sure, we had the hots for each other and I liked him a lot, but we hadn't even known each other two weeks.

"You got a circus going on behind your eyes there," Cass said. "Care to share?"

"No." It was embarrassing. My whole life was embarrassing these days. "But don't you think it's just a bit too good to be true? Cass meets a great guy, gets her memory back, saves the day. Now I've met a dude, am maybe getting my memory back…" I didn't even want to mention me saving the day. What if I couldn't? "I mean, it's all just too good to be true."

"Or maybe it's just time something started to go right," Cass said. "Face it, we've had a rough slog the last ten years. But it's only been getting better. Maybe things are finally, really, truly working out."

"Yeah." Nix nodded. "I like the sound of this. Because it means I'm next, and I want to meet my own smart, nice, hot dude and remember where the hell I'm from. So fess up to Roarke. Let's keep the good things coming."

A grin tugged at my lips. Maybe they were right. "Fine. I will. When the time is right. For now, I have to follow a mysterious map to who the hell knows what on the other end."

"Want us to come?" Nix asked.

"No," I said. "You guys gotta keep Ancient Magic going. We're going to need the money to pay back Mordaca and Aerdeca for the memory spells."

Cass grimaced. "Yeah, that wasn't cheap."

"You'd think they'd give us a discount because we're friends," Nix said.

Cass and I laughed at the absurdity. Aerdeca and Mordaca, giving discounts?

"If I really need you guys—like I know we've got a big fight ahead—I'll let you know," I said.

Nix grinned. "Good. I like our team outings."

"Team outings?" I asked. "Like a field trip?"

"Yeah, but more violent." Nix punched the air. "Keeps me in fighting shape."

I laughed. "I thought beating up the jerks who try to rob the shop did that."

"It does. Sorta. But they're easy targets. I like a challenge."

A challenge. I had a feeling that whatever was at the other end of this Guardian situation I was dealing with would probably be considered a challenge.

A big one.

CHAPTER NINE

It was with heavy footsteps that I made my way back up to my place. Would Roarke still be there? Did I owe him an apology?

Maybe. Probably.

Ah, hell, I'd have to figure it out.

When I opened the door and heard the shower running, my shoulders relaxed.

A reprieve.

I would take it.

I hurried into my bedroom, then into my trove. The piles of books, gleam of gold, and scatter of lucky charms calmed me. I ran my fingertips over a book that teetered on top of a pile as I went to a small chest that contained some of my favorite lucky charms.

It didn't take long to pick out a variety of lucky talismans. Four, to be precise. Two necklaces, a belt, and a bracelet. All were gold, which gave them a bit of extra lucky something, as far as I was concerned. It was more than I normally wore, but less than I wanted to, so I called it a victory. Semi-self-control for the win.

Wearing my battle gear, I returned to my bedroom just as the water shut off.

Whew. I planned to tell Roarke what I was, but I didn't want him catching me walking out of the wall as I exited my trove. Better to do it on my terms—not by being caught.

I gave him a moment to get dressed, then went out into the living room. He standing near the couch, tugging his shirt on as I entered.

His head popped over the top. "Hey."

"Hey." I stood awkwardly on my side of the room, not quite sure how I wanted to admit that I was wrong. To say it wasn't my favorite activity would be an understatement. "So, uh, maybe you have a point that there are some things I haven't been telling you."

"Yeah?"

"Yeah. But I have good reasons."

"I know."

And the thing was, he looked like he really *did* know. It made this easier.

"Well, anyway, I just wanted to let you know that I will tell you…stuff. That stuff I haven't been telling you, that is." Oh boy, I was handling this *super* well. This was why I normally stayed away from real relationships. "But let's just get this demon thing under control first, okay? I'm worried that the longer I hang out in one place, the more I'll attract. So I'd like to get a move on. That is, if you're still helping me."

His gaze softened, and he approached me. "I'm still helping you."

"Thank you." My heart thudded. "Really."

He leaned down and pressed a kiss to my forehead. I closed my eyes, savoring the touch.

When he pulled away, I couldn't make eye contact, so I walked to the window and peered out, unsurprised to see a demon out on the sidewalk, staring up at my window. He was muscular and tall, with pale yellow skin that made him look like a fit Minion. He was even bald. He just needed funny goggles and blue overalls.

Too bad he had a big old sword in his hand.

Great. This was just great.

"Another one?" Roarke asked.

"Yep."

Roarke came to join me at the window, standing far enough away that we didn't touch. But I could still feel the heat of him. I ignored it—tried to, at least—and focused on the fight below.

The green door that led to our apartments burst open, and Nix ran out, leaping up to deliver a flying kick to the demon's chest. The demon was so preoccupied with staring at my window that she landed the blow solidly. She'd always been best with hand-to-hand. A legacy of defending the shop from burglars for years.

The demon jumped to his feet, far more quickly than I'd have expected for a demon his size. Nix was unarmed, but I wasn't worried. She had this guy in the bag.

As expected, she ducked his sword blow, then kicked out and swept his legs out from under him. She was on him before he'd fully hit the ground, landing a mean punch to his jaw. She nailed him again, this time from the other side, and he passed out cold.

Nix jumped to her feet and dusted off her hands, then picked up the demon's blade and plunged it through his chest. She left the sword sticking upright, then leaned against Cass's old black car and watched the demon slowly disappear.

"You three are tough as nails," Roarke said.

"Yeah." Pride warmed my chest. "We are."

The closest Underpath portal to Cwm Y Ddraig was located about ten miles away near the walled castle town of Caernarfon. I followed Roarke out into a graveyard in the shadows of the castle wall, stumbling over a fallen headstone. Threatening clouds hung low overhead, crowding around the surrounding mountains and promising snow at any moment. Chill winter air froze my lungs and made my cheeks sting.

"At least it's daylight," Roarke said.

"No kidding." Because of the time change, we'd arrived here in daylight, thank fates.

I followed him through the tombstones toward the wrought iron fence. Just as we stepped out of the gate, a big black car pulled up, and a demon popped out. He'd pass for human among most people, but my new demon-savvy senses picked up his demonic nature from the strange gleam in his eyes.

"Just in time. Thank you, Florus," Roarke said.

Florus walked around the vehicle and handed Roarke the keys, his gaze glued on me.

"What's she?" Florus asked Roarke.

"None of your business, is what she is," Roarke said.

I eyed Florus warily, waiting to see what he would do. All demons weren't evil. So this one shouldn't necessarily attack me on sight. But I was so used to the other demons—the ones who usually served as mercenaries or who'd just recently escaped the Underworld. *They* were trouble.

Florus's nose twitched, as if he smelled something weird, then he turned to Roarke. "That all you need?"

"That's it for now, thanks. Give my best to your family."

Florus nodded and ambled off down the road, disappearing in a poof of gray smoke when he was about ten feet away.

"He's another one of your minions?"

"I prefer to think of them as staff," Roarke said as he climbed behind the wheel of the car.

I jumped in and sighed gratefully as warm air blasted from the heaters. "So how does it work? With the demons. He seemed much more…benign."

"I told you not all demons are evil."

"Yeah, I know." I'd literally *just* been thinking about it, but given my line of work, it was sometimes hard to remember. "But what's the deal with the ones who work for you? Do they live on Earth?"

He nodded as he pulled onto the narrow road and punched Cwm Y Ddraig into the GPS on the dash. "They do. They're demons who've proven to be trustworthy and valuable members of society. So I allow them to live on Earth with their families, scattered all over the globe, in return for their help in situations like this."

"Whoa." I turned to look at him as we drove out of the town surrounding the castle and into the woods. "So you bend the rules for them? Because demons aren't supposed to live on Earth. If they were, I'd be out of a job."

"You could still hunt treasure."

"True. But don't change the subject."

He grinned. "No. I don't break the rules. I have a special dispensation from the Order of the Magica. They agree that it's good to have some demons on our side."

Roarke slowed the car as the GPS told him to turn in twenty meters.

"Turn here," the dulcet tones of the GPS commanded.

But there was no road, just more trees.

Roarke turned anyway.

"Wait!" I pressed myself back into the seat.

Instead of plowing into a tree, the car bumped onto a tiny dirt road, and the vision of forest turned into a narrow lane, barely wide enough for our car.

"I'm going to guess the town of Cwm Y Ddraig isn't visible to humans." I glanced at the GPS unit in the dash. "So I assume the GPS lady is a supernatural."

Roarke grinned. We followed the tiny lane for about fifteen minutes before pretty slate buildings appeared ahead of us. Light glowed warmly in their windows, and snow sparkled on the bushes in front of the houses.

Demon Magic

The sound of a band of some kind—more the marching sort of band than the head-banging kind—echoed through the trees.

The houses that we passed were quiet, their dark slate roofs speckled with snow, but as we neared the center of town, the sound of revelers joined the music of the band.

"I think they're having a festival," I said as Roarke slowed the car to a crawl. We were near the center of town. Every inch of space around us was taken up by houses and gardens.

"What does your map say you're looking for?" Roarke asked.

I pulled the copy of the map that Nix had made for me out of my pocket and unfolded it. I didn't want to hurt the original. Nix's crazy good gift for conjuring meant that the replica was an exact match—perfect in every way. The best photocopier a girl could ask for.

I peered at the faded map for a moment, waiting for the letters to make sense.

"We're looking for the Eastern Rail," I said.

"Does it say where it's located? Or show a picture?"

"Nothing on the map. Give me a moment." I closed my eyes and called upon my dragon sense, hoping to catch something. But nothing tugged at my middle. No familiar feeling of direction. I just didn't know enough about the place. I tried to imagine what the old railway might have looked like and worked up every ounce of desire to find it that I could muster.

Still, I got nothing. Maybe I should have brought Cass or Nix along. Their stronger dragon sense would have helped.

"I have no idea," I said. "Though this town seems really small to have a train station."

We caught sight of the town square where colorful stalls were set up. In the middle, a band of about six played a jaunty tune. Dozens of people flocked between the stalls while thousands of twinkle lights glittered in the trees. The clouds were heavy enough overhead that the day was fairly dark, letting the twinkle lights really glow.

The mountains on the other side of town were daunting—black slate covered with patches of scrubby grass. Since most of the buildings were made of the same dark slate that formed the mountain, the place would be very bleak if it weren't for the colorful tents and sparkling lights.

Roarke parked the car on the street near the square and cut the engine. "We'll do the rest on foot. Poke around, ask the locals. It'll probably be faster than driving aimlessly."

I shoved the map back into my pocket and climbed out of the car, grateful for my warm hat and puffy coat. Though I hated to give up my black leather, Roarke had been right in suggesting the warmer alternative. North Wales in the winter was chilly.

We made our way toward the village square, passing warm pubs and closed teashops. The few people we passed were clearly supernaturals, though which type I couldn't determine. They looked human, except for their jewel-toned eyes and the magical signatures that hung heavy in the air.

We passed a few stalls before Roarke stopped at one selling hot cocoa out of a gleaming silver carafe. The chocolatey scent made my mouth water. A woman with rosy cheeks and a colorful patchwork coat smiled at us. She was about sixty, with the look that everyone recognized as *friendly mom*. I might not have had one of those, but even I knew what they looked like.

"From out of town, are you?" Her accent was thick as butter, and it took me a moment to figure out what the heck she had said.

"We are." Roarke grinned his most charming smile. "It's a lovely village."

The woman grinned back, and I had to admit, his smile worked on me too.

"It is, isn't it?" she said. "What can I get you?"

"Could we have two, please?" Roarke asked, nodding toward the gleaming silver carafe.

I glanced at him. The hot chocolate sounded divine—even now, my nose was freezing into an ice cube—but we were here to work.

"But of course you could, you handsome devil." The woman laid the flirt on thick as she prepared two takeaway cups, then passed them to us.

Roarke handed over the money and asked, "I don't suppose you know where the Eastern Railway is?"

The woman's gaze turned thoughtful. "No, dear. I'm sorry to say that the railway closed down about seventy years ago, so you're a bit late to catch a train."

"Really?"

"Oh yes. And anyhow, it didn't carry people. It carried slate from that mountain over there." She pointed toward the massive black mountain that crouched over the village like a dragon.

Maybe that's why I couldn't find the station. I'd been imagining a train full of people, not a train full of slate.

"But say we were interested just in seeing it," Roarke said. "Historical inquiry. How would we get there?"

He sold it so well that I totally bought it. We were definitely here on historical inquiry. Why wouldn't we be? Who *wouldn't* come to this lovely town to search for an old railway?

"Well now, that's an interesting subject. After the quarry closed down, so did the rail. Though you could find the remnants of the old track by the gin distillery. Very popular, that stuff. Making a real comeback. Artisanal gins." She nodded knowingly. "Just go around the building to the back, and you might be able to find remnants of the track. But be careful of the pixies, dear. They're liable to steal your hat."

"Which way is the distillery?" Roarke asked.

She pointed down the street. "Three blocks down, one over."

"Thank you."

She smiled. "You come back when you're done. Another chocolate on the house."

"Thank you," he repeated.

I grinned bemusedly at her, then up at Roarke.

He pointed down the street, the way the woman had directed, and said, "This way, then."

We hurried off, the warm cup of chocolate heating my hands. I took a sip and almost groaned at the chocolatey goodness.

"You bought the chocolate to make her friendlier, didn't you?" I asked.

"And because it smelled good." Roarke took a sip. "But yes. We didn't want to have to poke around too much, and you never know with tiny towns like these. Sometimes they don't like outsiders."

"True." We passed stalls selling savory meat pies, sausages, cakes, cookies, nuts, crafts, wooly hats, jewelry, and books. Everything you would want at a local fair.

"Do you have any idea what kind of supernaturals these are?" I whispered as we passed a group of shrieking schoolchildren who all had distinct jewel-toned eyes.

"No idea," Roarke said. "Strong magic, though."

We turned at the third block and went down one. The distillery was a small building with an artfully designed logo. It was quiet for the day no doubt the distillers having gone to join the party in the square.

We hurried around the building to the back. It butted up right to the woods. In the distance, the mountain glowered.

I almost groaned.

I'd bet big money that we'd be climbing that mountain before the day was over. I chucked my empty paper cup in the rubbish bin near the distillery's back door and set off toward the woods.

Roarke and I searched through the trees and bushes, our eyes glued to the ground. Finally, I caught sight of a burnished orange color. I leaned closer.

"I found it!" I poked the old iron track with my toe.

Roarke came to my side, and I pointed into the woods. "It leads that way. The map says it joins the Lake-So-Deep."

"Oh, good. Doesn't sound ominous at all."

I laughed, and we set off down the tracks, having to push our way through the bush occasionally. I could hear the chattering of the pixies in the forest around us, a high-pitched noise that was almost pleasant but wasn't. Warily, I reached up and held on to my hat. Tiny glowing eyes peered at me from the trees.

"I sure hope these are friendly pixies," I said.

"I'll scare 'em off." Roarke glowered at them, giving them his best scary face.

I laughed. "That was terrifying!"

We stepped through the trees a half second later to see something that actually *was* pretty terrifying. A mirror black lake with the black mountain looming behind it.

"Oh boy," I breathed. "You were right. It is ominous."

We made our way quickly across the clearing to the edge of the lake and looked out at the water. Snow began to fall, white and pure until it was swallowed by the lake, which looked a heck of a lot like oil. A hazy gray mist rose from the surface, floating high into the air.

I pulled the map from my pocket and peered at it.

"It says that a boat will take us across." I looked up, searching for a boat of any kind.

Roarke did the same. "I see nothing."

"It would have been seventy years ago. Or longer. It looks like we're too late."

On the other side of the lake, massive piles of discarded slate slid off the mountain, cutting off access to the strip of shore we needed. Walking around the lake and crossing the discarded slate would be too dangerous—there could be a rockslide. I didn't want to be crushed.

The mountain possessed the strangest topography I'd ever seen. Quarrying activities had turned it into a huge step pyramid, each level several hundred feet high. It was almost entirely black because the earth had been quarried straight down to the slate. Much of it had just been tossed aside, unused garbage. The only path up the mountain was between the two enormous piles of discarded slate, and the only way to get there was to cross the water somehow.

"I could fly us over," Roarke said.

"No." I glanced down at the map to confirm, then back at the lake, taking note of the black mist rising off of it. Birds circled the lake, but never flew over. Just like the map said. "We have to take a boat. There's a warning on the map. The lake is enchanted. The black mist that comes off the surface keeps anything from flying over. Look at the birds. Whatever is at the top of the mountain, they're determined to make you follow the map's directions to get there. No shortcuts."

Which was probably the real reason my dragon sense didn't work. Magic blocked it.

Roarke craned his neck, eventually finding the birds that I pointed to. None of them flew over the lake.

"There was more than just a slate quarry on that mountain," Roarke said.

I peered into the dark water of the lake. "And more than just fish in that water."

We needed a boat. I'd raised one before. I could do it again. If there was one in there. "I've got an idea. Give me a sec."

I shoved the map back in my pocket and closed my eyes. I didn't know what period of boat might be sunk in that lake, but I hoped it didn't matter. With a deep breath, I called upon my magic, trying to ignore the block that was supposed to be placed upon my mind. I couldn't feel it, but the knowledge that it was there was unpleasant.

I could totally do this. Practice, practice, practice, like Draka had said in my dream. Just because it was unreliable didn't mean it was impossible.

Magic sparked inside of me, a bright light that I tried to reach. I strained, desperate to catch it, as I envisioned a boat rising from the depths of the black lake. Power vibrated on the air. *My* power.

I wasn't going to let some damned curse stop me. I didn't want to live like this—only able to use my magic occasionally and if I got lucky.

"Whoa." Roarke's soft exhalation made me open my eyes.

A dirty wooden boat was rising out of the water, its decks covered in seaweed. The middle was broken apart, the wood splintered. I envisioned the timbers knitting themselves back together and the weeds sinking back below the surface of the lake.

Slowly, the boat did as I requested, then floated toward the shore. When it beached, the air over the deck began to shimmer. A man's hazy outline formed.

Shit.

I didn't want to have to deal with some miner from 1910.

I reeled my magic in, shoving it back inside of me. The man's outline disappeared, leaving only the boat.

"Not bad," Roarke said.

"Let's just hope it lasts."

I approached the boat, which was about twenty feet long with a wide, flat deck. Perfect for stacking cargo. A ragged sail hung from the mast, but four massive paddles were stacked against the side of the hull. For low-wind situations. Or for when you brought the ship up from the bottom of the lake and the sail was still in crap condition.

I climbed aboard, my feet squishing on the wood, which was still partially water-logged. Weeds scattered the deck here and there. "Not exactly in mint condition."

Roarke stepped aboard. "It's got a bit of Davy Jones clinging to it, but it'll do."

"I don't think that sail is going to pick up any wind." I eyed the massive holes in the fabric, then went and picked up two of the heavy paddles. I handed one to Roarke. "This might take a while."

The lake was pretty wide. At least four hundred yards across.

We took up position on either side of the boat and began to paddle. There was no sun because of the snow clouds, but the water gleamed all the same. It was eerie.

The going was slow, and by the time we were halfway across, my muscles ached. I was glad he was here. I'd never have managed to row across by myself.

I stopped rowing and wheezed, "Break time."

Roarke stopped paddling, and we sat dead still on the lake as I heaved to catch my breath.

Around us, the black water began to ripple, little waves that popped up out of nowhere. Magic sparked on the air, smelling like dead seaweed.

Roarke eyed the waves. "There's no wind."

"Yeah." I plunged my oar back into the water, my heart starting to pound from more than just exhaustion. "This is weird. Let's go."

We'd barely taken a stroke before something massive plunged into the side of the boat. I stumbled, falling to my knees.

"Del! Look--" Roarke's shout was cut off by another massive crash.

Something pushed the boat from underneath, flipping it up and over.

I crashed into the water, the freezing cold stealing my breath and sending an icepick of pain through my head. I flailed, trying to determine up and down. I opened my eyes, only able to see the tiniest glow of light. I followed the bubbles that escaped my mouth, kicking upward and stretching for the surface, only to crash into the wooden boat above.

It had capsized and was sinking! The heavy wood pushed me deeper into the water. Frantic, I kicked to the side, trying to escape the heavy press of the boat. I'd nearly reached the edge when something grabbed my ankle and pulled me deeper.

Water monster!

I screamed, losing the last of my precious air. The grip tightened as I kicked and thrashed. At best, I had a minute before I lost consciousness.

Fighting instinct kicked in, driving away the panic. I called on my Phantom form. No icy chill raced through me like it usually did. The water made me too cold for that. But my skin turned blue and transparent, lighting up the water with a glow.

A bubbly shrieking sound tore through the water, and the grip on my ankle loosened. The water monster was affected by my Phantom touch!

But my lungs still burned from lack of air. Even as a Phantom, I needed to breathe. Weakening, I kicked for the surface, wishing I was a fish shifter or something.

I'd only made it a few feet when the monster grabbed me again. It hissed, but held on, clearly desperate for this catch if he was willing to grab me.

I kicked and fought for the surface, but its grip was too strong. Panic squeezed my throat as I reached for the sword strapped to my back. The smooth, familiar grip of the hilt calmed me as I yanked it free and doubled over.

I couldn't kill the thing while touching it. I didn't want to inherit a water monster's power. What if I developed an unquenchable desire to drown people? But I could try to wound it until it let me go.

My blue Phantom glow lit up the water below, shining upon the horrifying, gilled face of the water monster that had grabbed me. It was vaguely human shaped, with spindly limbs and a face like some kind of fish. Weeds waved in the water behind the monster, right in front of the gaping black mouth of a cave.

We were almost to its lair.

I swallowed my panic and swept out with my blade, my strike slow because of the water. I aimed for the arm that grabbed me. Just before the blade connected with the monster, I turned corporeal, allowing the blade to connect. The water turned dark without the blue glow of my Phantom form, but I felt the steel slice through flesh.

The grip on my ankle loosened.

I kicked for the surface, but it grabbed me again. With my lungs burning, I returned to Phantom form. Though my glow lit the water, blackness crept in at the edges of my vision.

I was nearly out of air.

Only seconds left.

I called upon my ice magic, praying it would work, and sent an icicle spear at the monster's stomach. Magic sparked in the water as it shot forth and pierced the monster. The grip around my ankle loosened, and I kicked for the surface.

But I was too weak. The water felt like quicksand. No matter how hard I tried, my lungs and muscles burning, I only sank deeper into the water. When I hit the hard, flat bottom of the lake, my vision was almost entirely blacked out.

CHAPTER TEN

With the last of my strength, I turned my head to see if I'd gotten the damned monster. It was floating in the water, the ice spear through its middle. Not dead yet, but eventually.

Out of the corner of my eye, I caught sight of the flat wooden deck of the boat. Hope flared.

I wasn't on the bottom of the lake! The hard surface beneath me was the boat.

Though I had no physical strength left, I had my magic. I called upon it, more desperate than I'd ever been in my entire life. If I couldn't make it work, I was dead.

Or something.

How many lives could I have? I'd probably go back to the Underworld, and I didn't want to do that.

My magic sparked within me as I attempted to bring the boat back to life, allowing it to float again.

My magic resisted, too weak. Or I was too weak, unable to control it. I envisioned Draka, her comforting hand on my shoulder as she told me to believe in myself.

I didn't realize it was working until the water began to flow by my face and a brighter glow appeared above me. We were rising! The boat was heading toward the surface with me aboard.

By the time the boat broke through, I was so desperate for air that I sucked it in too early, taking a mouthful of lake water. I coughed, rolling over and retching, until I could gasp the cold, clear air into my lungs. My vision cleared and strength returned to my muscles, though I shivered with such ferocity that it felt like my bones might snap. Snow still fluttered down, sticking to my wet clothes and hair.

As soon as I could move, I scrambled to my feet and shoved my blade back into the holster that was still clinging to my back. I spun in a circle, searching for Roarke.

"Roarke!" I choked out, my throat still raw from retching.

About ten yards away, the water splashed as two figures thrashed. I could just make out Roarke's dark head and the slimy green figure of another lake monster. Roarke broke the thing's neck, then flung it away from him. Another water monster's body floated nearby. He'd killed two, so that made at least three. I hoped there were no more.

"Over here!" I waved my arms.

He spun to face me, his head bobbing above the black surface, then kicked his way toward me, swimming with powerful strokes. He climbed aboard, shivering as hard as I was. His dark hair was plastered to his scalp, and his skin was the color of flour. The black of his eyes stood out starkly.

"This is a problem." He shuddered hard.

I sat hard on the deck, so cold that my muscles were unable to hold me.

"Yeah," I said. We could freeze to death out here. Why hadn't I stolen a fire demon's power?

Roarke sat next to me, wrapping a long arm around my shoulders. The faintest bit of warmth flowed from him to me, but he was just as much of an ice block as I was.

"I really don't want to have to go back and get warm clothes," I said, unsure of whether or not we'd even make it back.

I looked around the boat, searching for the paddles. We had to get a move on, either way.

My heart dropped. "The paddles are gone. They must have fallen off when the boat capsized."

"Shit." Roarke rubbed his forehead.

We were stuck in the middle of the lake, two hundred meters from shore in either direction, and Roarke couldn't even fly us out of here.

The water splashed off the bow and I stiffened.

"Another monster?" Roarke stood.

"I'll beg your pardon!" An offended feminine voice sounded from the water.

I glanced toward it just as a beautiful woman climbed aboard. She wore a sparkling white dress and pearls in her long, dark hair. Without a doubt, she was the most gorgeous person I'd ever seen in my life.

And she was out for a swim?

I stood. "Who are you?"

"Morwena. I am a Morgen." She roamed the boat, inspecting it.

I searched my mind for any memory of a Morgen. Were they some kind of water sprite?

"Normally I would kill you for daring to trespass on my lake," she said. "But you've assisted me greatly by killing the Afanc."

"Is that what those sea monsters were?"

"Yes." She turned to face us, her green eyes blazing. "They've been a nuisance for fifty years. The lake is well rid of them."

I shivered hard, hoping she would get to the point. We needed to get out of here. Somehow.

She stepped forward, holding out a hand. Her magic surged on the air, smelling like a rainstorm. Warmth radiated from her palm, drying my clothes immediately and sinking into my muscles and bones. They turned to jelly right away, the most amazing feeling in the world. I almost plopped down on my butt. It took all my strength to keep standing. One glance at Roarke showed that he was dry, too, his color no longer deadly pale.

"Thank you," I said.

"You humans are so fragile about the cold," she said. "Why are you upon my lake? No one has ventured here in decades."

I pointed to the other side. "We need to go there."

"Whatever for? There is nothing there anymore."

"We need to get to the top."

Her brows rose. "Are you sure you want to do that?"

Her tone made me nervous. "Why? What's up there?"

She shrugged. "Nothing…lately."

I waited for her to elaborate, but she didn't. "Can you tell us more about what was up there?"

"No. But I can give you advice."

"We'll take it." I nodded encouragingly.

She pointed to the strip of land that we wanted to reach. The mountain rose up steeply behind it. There were at least ten massive land steps where the mountain rose up, then leveled off. Then rose and leveled, rose and leveled.

"Do you see the stone ramps between each flat level?" she asked.

I squinted, finally able to make out the huge ramps made of slate. They were black, like the rest of the mountain, and hard to distinguish, but they were there. One ramp connected each of the flat areas of land, upon which sat old buildings. It looked like you could climb up the mountain by sticking to the ramps, getting higher with every level.

"I see them," I said.

"Those ramps were built for the tram system that transported the slate and the workers. There are railroad tracks built onto them that would carry the mining carts. They lead all the way up the mountain. Follow the tracks. Do not deviate, or you will anger the Coblynau."

"Coblynau?"

"Mining goblins. They used to assist the miners. Since operations have been shut down, they have been…bored. You do not want to provide them with a diversion, because I promise you will not like it. They can kill you with a touch, if they so choose."

"With a touch?" I asked.

"Yes. Even you." Her gaze was knowing. "Phantom."

She must've seen me shift in the water.

"But nothing can kill me in Phantom form."

"There, you are wrong," she said. "The Coblynau's touch is deadly to *all*. And you must not kill them. They will only multiply and become enraged."

Kill *me* with a touch? Multiply? Yikes.

"Thank you," Roarke said.

"Thank you for killing the Afanc." She turned to the stern of the boat and waved her hand at the water. It surged, pushing the boat forward.

"That's awesome," I said.

She smiled as she directed us closer to our destination. "It is, rather."

As the mountain loomed ever closer, the sheer size of the place became more apparent. The ramps were longer than football fields and at least twenty meters wide. The buildings on each of the flat portions of land looked long abandoned.

"All this for slate?" I asked. "It has to be the biggest mine in the world."

"Not just for slate," Morwena said.

"What else?"

She shrugged. "Other things."

The boat beached, the bow shoving up onto the shore. I jumped down, grateful to be off the water, and turned back. "Thank you."

She nodded. "Remember. Stick to the tracks."

"We will." Roarke jumped down beside me.

Morwena waved, then leapt off the boat into the water. She disappeared beneath the black surface without a splash.

"That was good luck." I pulled the map from my pocket, unfolded it, and scanned the contents. "It mentions a *Path Red as Rust*. That must be the railroad tracks that Morwena mentioned. We're supposed to follow it to the *Great Black Mouth*."

"Great Black Mouth?" Roarke frowned. "A cave?"

"Yeah, maybe."

I turned to search for the tracks, finding them quickly on the bare beach. They were the rusty iron red of the ones in the woods on the other side of the lake, but there was nothing to obscure them here on the beach.

I set off toward them, Roarke at my side.

He looked up at the first ramp. "That thing is enormous."

I nodded, climbing up onto it. The angle was steep—at least forty degrees—but the slate that had been used to build it was still well stacked. It was an incredible piece of architecture.

We began to climb. I leaned my weight forward so as not to fall backward, and kept behind Roarke who was faster than me. Soon, I was huffing and puffing, my lungs burning. Beneath my hat, my hair began to sweat. I pulled the hat off and shoved it in my pocket, grateful for the cool air on my head.

We made it to the first flat level, which was carpeted with yellowed grass. A building sat at the top of the ramp, housing a large piece of rusty machinery with broken metal cables hanging out of a massive wheel thing.

"That must be the pulley system that raised and lowered the mining carts," I said.

Roarke nodded, then pointed to the rusty railroad track that turned left, heading toward another huge ramp that sat fifty yards away. "That way."

I followed him, sticking to the track, which occasionally disappeared beneath the grass. We passed a couple more roofless and doorless buildings built of slate. I craned my neck to see inside, spotting rusty table saws that looked like they could cut through my motorcycle. Scooter wouldn't like that. But they must have been for cutting the slate before sending it down the mountain.

We began the hike up the second ramp, then the third and fourth. Despite the light snowfall, I was sweating like an old guy in a sauna, my jacket unzipped and my scarf shoved in my pocket.

"Think we're almost there?" I wheezed.

Mist shrouded the mountain above, lending it a threatening air.

"Not even close," Roarke said.

An eerie laugh sounded from a building to our left. I spun just in time to see a sheep run out of the building, hurtling toward us on spindly black legs. I dodged, barely missing its fluffy body, and stumbled in the grass.

"Del!" Roarke grabbed my arm and pulled me back onto the tracks, but it was too late.

The laughing sound increased, followed by the scuttling of footsteps on the slate around us.

"The Coblynau," I said, just as twelve gobliny-looking creatures jumped out from behind piles of slate.

They were about four feet tall and horribly ugly, wearing old-time miners' clothing. Their eyes and fingertips glowed green. Was that their power to kill with a touch? And Morwena said they would multiply if we killed them. Crap.

"We can't hurt them."

"Run," Roarke said.

We set off down the tracks. I sprinted behind Roarke, my muscles burning. The climb up nearly killed me, but the Coblynau were slower than us because of their short legs. Just barely.

When I turned back, we were nearly at the top. I leapt onto flat ground just in time to see another group of Coblynau pop up on the hill above. They stood on a massive pile of discarded slate right overhead.

Their laughter grew as they began to push and kick the slate. It slipped and slid.

My heart leapt into my throat. "They're trying for a rockfall!"

"I'll shift."

But there was no time. Before Roarke could call upon his magic, the massive pile of slate began to slide down. There was a tiny round building right in front of us. It had massively thick walls and was the only building we'd seen with a roof still remaining. The roof itself was a domed shape, formed by slate that was several feet thick.

I shoved Roarke toward it, diving inside behind him just as thousands of pounds of slate crashed down around us, cutting out all light. Dust billowed in from the entrance to the little hut. I coughed, then sat up.

I called upon my Phantom magic, using my ghostly blue glow to illuminate the building. It was even smaller on the inside, a tiny round space that barely fit the two of us.

"Quick thinking." Roarke stood. Mostly. He had to crouch because the ceiling was so low.

"Maybe," I said, suddenly doubting my actions. What if I'd trapped us forever?

"What the hell is this place?" Roarke asked.

I inspected it, catching sight of something on the ground. I knelt to get a better look, discovering an old fuse for dynamite along with a wire that led out of the building.

"I think it was a blast house. I've read about these." I pointed to the equipment. "They'd blow up parts of the mountain to get at the slate. But they'd hide in here while they did it, so they didn't get crushed."

Roarke reached up and touched the ceiling. "Glad this place held up, then."

"Yeah." I stood and went to the entrance. Jagged pieces of slate formed a wall of indeterminate thickness. Who knew how big this pile of rock was?

"I'm going to walk through it in my Phantom form," I said. "Maybe I can move the rocks."

"No." Roarke's voice was sharp. "Morwena said the Coblynau can kill you even in your Phantom form. You wouldn't have time before they got to you."

"Then what do we do? Do you think you can blast us out of here?"

Roarke shrugged. "I'm going to have to try."

I flattened myself against the back wall, and Roarke went to the entrance. His magic filled the hut, the taste of wine and the smell of sandalwood growing strong, which just made me think—*what I wouldn't give for a mug of my boxed wine and a few hours on my couch right now...*

The tornado of black mist formed around Roarke. A moment later, he stood transformed, his clothing gone and replaced with an expanse of dark gray muscle and massive wings. Though he folded them in toward himself and crouched down, there was still barely enough room for the two of us.

He spoke in his gravelly demon voice as he turned to me. "If we manage this, be ready to run. It's not going to be quiet, and the Coblynau will notice."

I nodded.

He turned back to the entrance. His magic surged again as he heaved his fist back and then punched the wall of slate. The stone exploded outward, and my heart leapt.

But no daylight flooded in.

Roarke walked into the hole he'd created, but it was barely anything at all.

"Too much slate to go that way," he said.

Damn.

"Come here." He gestured to me.

I stood and walked to him. He scooped me up in his arms, clutching me to his chest.

"What the heck?" I asked.

"We're going through the roof. But you have to come with me, or you'll be crushed by the falling rock once the roof is destroyed."

"I can just go through as a Phantom," I said.

"I know." His brows drew together and he hesitated. "It's just that…when I'm near you—touching you—my power is enhanced."

"What?" That sounded crazy.

"I don't know if it's because of what you are and the fact that I'm the Warden of the Underworld, but contact with you increases my power."

That was weird. I'd have to unpack and examine that later. "Um, okay, then. But do you think busting out through the roof will work?"

"I hope so."

It was better than me trying to fight off the Coblynau while trying to dig him out, so I nodded and curled up against his chest, trying to make myself as small as possible.

Roarke crouched low to the ground, his wings wrapped around us so that we formed a bullet-like shape, then pushed off with a massive surge of force.

We hurtled upward, crashing through the roof and up into the sky. The blast of slate was enormous, scattering the stuff all over the mountain. When we began to fall, Roarke extended his wings, a groan of pain escaping him as he did so.

I looked up, catching sight of his wings, torn and tattered. Blood poured down his forehead and dripped from his wings.

Oh shit.

His wings slowed our descent to the ground, but there was no way he could fly. I just hoped he could walk. We landed with a thud, Roarke stumbling to his knees.

I leapt out of his arms and knelt in front of him, tilting his chin up. His face was covered in blood. His wings were a broken mess behind him.

"I thought magic protected you when you broke through things like this!" I cried. "You tore through Tintagel Castle with no problem!"

"It protects me...mostly." He swayed on his feet. "That was a lot...of jagged slate."

Laughter sounded around us, growing louder and closer. I glanced up. The Coblynau—a dozen of them, at least—leapt out from behind piles of slate and slid down the loose rocks toward us.

"We gotta go," I said.

Roarke staggered to his feet, but was slow.

One of the miserable little goblins was nearly to us. My skin chilled. I couldn't let him touch us!

I shot him with an icicle. It threw him back about twenty feet, but when he finally stood, another Coblynau appeared right next to him.

The doubling that Morwena had mentioned.

Damn it.

"Can you run?" I asked Roarke as I shot another Coblynau, willing to duplicate a few of them if it meant keeping them off us long enough for Roarke to recover.

He nodded, straightening and stretching. "Yeah, let's go."

We sprinted off, tumbling and sliding down the pile of slate until we found the metal tracks again. We raced along them and up another ramp, into the mist that shrouded the very top of the mountain.

The Coblynau followed, their eerie laughter attracting more of their kind. It was hard to see them through the mist. It was hard to see anything. Visibility had been cut to only twenty feet.

We gained speed as Roarke recovered, sprinting up the last bit of ramp and turning left, following the track.

For fate's sake, I hoped we were near the top! I knocked on my head for good measure, nearly missing the fact that the track disappeared into thin air in front of us.

Roarke grabbed my arm, yanking me to a halt.

"Shit." My eyes popped out as I took in the old iron track disappearing into empty space. The ground beneath the track had fallen away at some point, leaving nothing but air. The track had followed, and now hung eerily off into nothingness. Forty feet away, the ground started up again. I could even see a bit of track on that side.

But there was no way to get there. Just a massive pit in the middle from a rockfall.

I glanced at Roarke, whose wings hung limply behind him.

The Coblynau's laughter grew louder.

Double shit.

"I can try to fly," Roarke said.

"We'd fall out of the sky."

It was one thing to bring a boat up out of the water. It was entirely another to bring back a mountain. That was too much. Far too difficult.

An idea sparked.

It was only forty feet across. I could do this. I had to do this.

Ice was just a Cat 2 power. Easier to manipulate. It would work.

I knocked on my head, then called upon my ice power, letting it fill me with its shivery cold. When I felt full to bursting, I pressed my hand to the track and sent a blast of ice outward, envisioning a bridge.

Let it goooooo! I sang in my head as the glittery blue ice shot across the open air, forming a bridge with the other side. It was a few feet wide and at least as thick. It would hold.

I hoped.

I stood. "Let's do this."

Roarke glanced doubtfully at me, then shook his head and started across, leading the way. After the first few tentative steps, we started to run. I slipped once, nearly plummeting off the side, but Roarke caught me. The Coblynau's laughter echoed behind us, bouncing off the mountain and echoing.

Goosebumps prickled my skin and fear chilled my blood. There was nothing below us except open space and jagged rock a thousand feet below. Just my magic.

Sweat broke out on my skin as we sprinted the last half. When my feet finally hit solid ground, my knees turned to rubber.

Roarke turned, kneeling and raising his fist. He punched the bridge with one big fist, sending his magic through it. The ice shattered, sending the Coblynau plummeting.

He turned to me and we ran, racing along the track. We reached another ramp and scrambled up. The eerie laughter of the Coblynau grew. They climbed out from crevices in the rock from all around us. More and more. The whole mountain was teeming with them.

There would be no fighting them. Only running.

I thought my heart would explode by the time we reached the top. A decrepit iron mining cart sat there, long abandoned after carrying its last load of slate down the tracks to the lake.

I dodged around it, catching sight of the mouth of the cave in front of us, perched on the cliff.

We'd made it! The *Great Black Mouth*. A cave, just like Roarke had guessed.

The Coblynau's laughter and their scrambling footsteps sounded louder.

"Hurry," Roarke said.

We hurtled toward the cave entrance, darting inside. I spun around to look out. The Coblynau crested the top of the ramp and caught sight of us, their eyes brightening.

Shit!

I called upon my magic, nearly drained, praying that I had enough. As the Coblynau sprinted toward us, the ice filled my chest and limbs. I touched the cave wall near the entrance, willing the ice to fill it like a wall. It grew outward from the rock, glittering and bright, closing us in like that weird circular door on the spaceship in the movie *Independence Day*.

The Coblynau reached us just as it closed. They beat their fists against the ice, but it was at least two feet thick. I lowered my hand, panting. I'd used up almost every ounce of magic I had and was running on fumes. I'd need to rest to regenerate.

Somehow, I doubted I'd have the opportunity.

"That should buy us some time," Roarke said.

"Yeah." I stepped back, sticking my tongue out at the goblins.

They shrieked, enraged, their eyes and fingertips glowing green. I turned, joining Roarke, who still looked like hell covered in blood with tattered wings.

"Now what?" He wiped some of the blood off his face with his hands, but it didn't help much.

I pulled the map out of my pocket, unfolded it, and read by the light that flowed through the ice wall.

"They wait in the darkness broken only by the fall of the water," I read.

"That's obscure."

"No kidding." I started forward. "Let's go figure it out."

We set off through the dark. A faint blue glow shined from the black slate walls, just enough that we could see where we were going.

"Thanks for getting us out of that blast house," I said.

"No problem."

"Sorry you got so badly hurt."

He grinned and looked down at himself, hoisting his wings up a bit. He winced at the motion, but said, "This? It's nothing."

"Yeah, sure." Nix and Cass were right. He'd more than proved he had my back. I should trust him with my secrets.

We walked in silence for a while. The tunnel was about as wide and tall as a school bus and very uniform. Eventually, splattering water sounded in the distance.

When we walked out into a massive cavern lit by a silvery blue waterfall, my jaw nearly dropped. The water glowed, shedding a hazy light over the cave. Blue lights glittered against the ceiling high above. Gold ore was piled high against the walls, thousands of pounds of it. My dragon sense lit up immediately, making my fingertips itch to go touch the stuff.

Touch it. Hell, I wanted to dive in it like Scrooge McDuck.

"Whoa…" I murmured. "They weren't just mining slate."

"My thoughts exactly." Roarke strode to the pool of water and knelt beside it to wash the blood from his face.

I explored while he cleaned up, desperately trying to ignore the gold while looking for the exit. There was none.

Which meant this was our destination.

But no one waited here.

I pulled out the map and consulted it again. There was nothing new on it.

When I looked up, Roarke was mostly clean and had shifted back into his human form. Thank fates he was powerful enough that his clothes had reappeared. I was already starting to get cold again now that we weren't running for our lives.

"Where are they?" I asked. "No one is here."

"This is the end?"

"Yeah." I paced, searching for any sign of life. "I don't know what I expected, but it wasn't this."

The waterfall tumbling into the little lake was glorious. So was the general feel of this place, all misty and blue.

But that it was empty except for the gold.

And I had basically no magical juice left to bring this place back to life and see what had once been here. There was no way I could turn back time right now. Not the way I was feeling. My magic was just dregs. I continued to pace, eyeing every inch of the cave like it held the secrets of the universe.

"What do you think those look like?" I pointed to four big slate rocks on the other side of the pool. They were roughly square.

"Pedestals?"

"Yeah, that's what I was thinking." I walked closer to the water to get a better look. My gaze caught on three dark blue spots deep in the pool. I squinted at them. "Did you see those earlier?"

"See what?" Roarke joined me and peered into the water. "I just see water."

"Really? Not dark blue orbs?"

"No orbs."

Huh. They were definitely orbs. I pulled the sword off my back and stripped out of my jacket, then toed off my boots. "I'm going in. But you're not allowed to look."

"Not allowed?"

"I'm not gonna wear my clothes in, crazy." I shivered at the memory of being soaking wet on the deck of the boat.

"What if something happens to you in there? I can't exactly let you jump in a magical pool alone."

"Sure you can. Anyway, I'm the only one who can see them. And I have a feeling that if this is some kind of challenge, then I need to be the one to complete it. Isn't that how quests work? I'm seeking the answers, so I have to pass the test."

He nodded. "Yeah, fair enough. But I at least need to know if you need help."

"Fine. I'll wear my underwear. No staring." At least I was wearing conservative stuff. I wasn't the sort to go on quests in scratchy lace underwear.

Anymore. I'd learned that lesson the hard way.

He grinned. "Deal."

I stripped down to my simple black bra and underpants. Roarke kept his gaze on the water, but I couldn't help but blush. Today really wasn't going the way I'd expected.

Scratch that. The details might be a bit off, but the reality was—standing here in my underwear in a weird cave, clueless and cold, wasn't that much of a surprise.

I adjusted the straps on my sword sheath and strapped it over my back.

"You're taking that underwater?"

"Never know when I'm going to need it." Though I now had the ice magic to help out, I was running on magical fumes.

I poked a toe in the water, grateful to find that it was at least temperate, then plunged in. With a deep breath, I dove deep. The water sizzled and bubbled around me, hot at my back. When something molten dripped onto my skin, I shrieked and thrashed, tearing my sword sheath off.

When I opened my eyes, I saw the metal of my sword melting out of the sheath, dripping to the pebbled lakebed.

Shit!

I kicked for the surface, breaking through and gulping air.

"What the hell was that?" Roarke demanded.

"My sword melted!" Damn it. I'd loved that sword.

"Get out of the water."

"No." I had to get those shining blue spheres. I was certain of it. "I have to do this, Roarke."

His gaze hardened. "I will come in and get you."

"You better not." I peered into the water, taking stock of my location in relation to the orbs. I was close to one. Right over it. "I'm going back down."

Before he could say anything, I dove deep and opened my eyes. Everything was sparkly and blue. I kicked downward, heading toward the closest blue orb.

It sparkled as I neared, a perfect sphere of glass. I poked it with a finger. When it didn't burn or shock me, I picked it up. The thing had to weigh thirty pounds if it weighed an ounce. My lungs burned as I kicked for the surface. When my head broke through, I gasped, then swam for the closest shore.

It was the one opposite where Roarke stood, with the pedestal-like things.

I heaved the orb onto the shore, then returned to the water twice more, retrieving the other two orbs. I was panting by the time I crawled out of the water, ready for a drink and a nap.

As I staggered to my feet, I studied the four pedestals. If only there had been four glass orbs. It'd have been obvious to put them on the four pedestals. I approached the pedestals anyway, catching sight of indentions on each one.

Might as well try. I made quick work of stacking an orb on each pedestal. When the last was finally in place, the air in the cavern vibrated.

"Whoa." I stumbled back from the pedestals, up to my ankles in the water.

The air vibrated so strongly that the glass orbs shattered. Blue mist exploded from them, coalescing to form three massive figures.

Phantom dragons. As big as a house and right in front of me.

CHAPTER ELEVEN

Standing here in my underwear in front of three Phantom dragons had to be the anti-highlight of my day.

Especially when they roared. The deafening sound echoed through the chamber, blasting my eardrums.

I stumbled back, falling on my butt in the water.

My heart leapt into my throat, and I scrambled deeper, away from them. I could tell immediately that none of them were Draka. One stalked forward, its transparent shimmery scales gleaming as it loomed over me with its great jaw hanging open.

"I'm supposed to be here!" I cried. "I mean no harm!"

The water splashed behind me. Roarke jumping in to come save me, if I had to bet. But I didn't dare take my eyes off the Phantom dragons.

"No! Go back!" I shouted to him. They wouldn't want outsiders nearby.

The dragon above me roared louder. Yep. They didn't like him coming closer.

The splashing from behind stopped. The dragon leaned over me until its great blue eyes were level with my own. Distrust gleamed in their depths.

I swallowed hard, sweat breaking out on my skin.

Why was this happening? I had the map. I was supposed to be here!

I had to show them I was one of them. But I was utterly drained. Managing even an ounce of magic sounded impossible.

Not that I had a choice.

I had to turn Phantom-ghosty or get chomped.

I called on the last of my power, letting the icy magic of my Phantom gift flow through me. It took a long, stressful moment to catch on, but my skin turned blue and transparent.

The dragon backed off, its gaze considering.

I stood on shaky legs. "I'm Delphine Bellator. I had a map that led me here."

A tense moment passed. I held my breath.

Finally, blue light swirled around the three dragons, and they transformed into human-shaped Phantoms wearing long, simple robes. Just like Draka. Each possessed timeless features. Mostly human, a little bit not. I thought one might've been a man, but I wasn't sure.

The one who felt the oldest approached. I had no idea how she *felt* old, but she just did.

"You may stand." Her voice was smooth and deep.

"Uh, okay." I stood on shaky legs, glancing behind me to check on Roarke.

He stood in the water up to his waist, frozen in place, his gaze riveted to us. Smart man. It definitely wouldn't please the dragons if a non-Phantom got involved.

I turned back to the Phantoms. "So, um, I'm here for some answers. About controlling my magic. But...but who are you?"

Wow, I was handling this smoothly.

The woman smiled. She was so transparent that I could make out the details of the slate wall behind her. "We are the last of the Phantom dragons, and we have been waiting for you for a long time, Guardian."

"Me?"

Oh fates. There was that Guardian thing again. Just like what Draka had called me. "Is Draka one of you? Where is she?"

"She is our fourth. But we don't know where she has gone or what has happened to her. Something knocked our vessels off the pedestals. Draka's vessel disappeared then. We don't know where she is."

That sucked. Worry gnawed at my chest. "Is she in danger?"

"Perhaps."

Damn. "But that's why you were in the lake, then?"

"Yes. The Coblynau protect us, normally. It should be impossible to reach us here. Except for you, because you had the map."

Double damn. "So if I'm supposed to be able to reach you, that means you can help me get control of my power? Because I'm having a hell of a time controlling my new Ubilaz demon power."

She nodded. "Yes. That is a particularly difficult one to control. Worse, the curse upon your mind makes it impossible."

"Who cursed me? How do I get rid of it?"

"The Shadows cursed you. Your goals are directly opposed to theirs. But the curse has been breaking down with time—you've been overcoming it. First by perfecting your ability to transport when you were a child, and then by practicing with your Phantom magic and ice magic. Some types of magic come more naturally to you than others, of course."

"Of course?" She was losing me.

"Yes. That which you were born with. The Phantom magic and the transporting, specifically. Stolen powers are much more difficult to manage. But we have something that will help you. A talisman." She walked to the water and knelt, laying her palm flat upon the glittering blue surface. Her blue robe floated on the lake around her, glimmering in the light.

The water glowed bright from the very deepest part of the lake. Instinctually, I stepped out of the water and watched. The glow became almost blinding until it coalesced into a tight little spot and zipped through the water toward the Phantom. She gripped something shiny and stood, then handed it to me.

I stared at the gleaming sword hilt in her hand. There was no blade, just the hilt, and it was decorated with incredible inscriptions of some kind.

"Is that my sword?" I asked.

"Not the one that you so carelessly wore into our water, no." She thrust it toward me, and I took it.

As soon as I clasped my hand around the metal, it felt as natural as if I'd been born with it in my hand. "Then what is it?"

"It is yours. Your Phantom blade. It will become part of you when it is whole. A talisman that will help you focus and control your power."

"But there's no blade."

She smiled. "No. Nothing is ever easy."

"You call getting here easy?"

Her smile didn't falter. "You are near to the end, but you have farther yet to go. You must find the other part of the sword and prove yourself worthy of it. The hilt gives you partial control of your magic. Manipulating the past will be easier now because you've practiced it before. But the blade will complete the circle, giving you control of magic that you've failed with. Such as the demons."

"Where do I find the blade?"

"I do not know, or we would have it. You are the only one who can find it. Use your gift. Once you've joined the two halves, you'll have full control of your magic. This blade will become a part of you—forged with your mind and body. You'll be able to kill demons with it, stealing their powers only when you desire. And it won't require a sheath. It can be stored within the ether and will appear to you whenever you need it."

"That would be handy." In fact, all of that sounded *very* good. I'd loved my old sword, but this one felt just as good in my hand. Better even. And it had some badass upgrades. "But if my dragon—" I cut myself off, remembering at the last minute that Roarke was listening

"If my gift didn't work to help me find this place, will it work to find the blade? Or do I need a map for that, too?"

"No. Your sense will work. Our cave is protected from any who seek us using anything but the approved map. We didn't want just anyone wandering in here."

"Right. Of course. So, I'm just supposed to leave here and assume I can find the blade to this sword?" I held the hilt up.

"Yes. When you are ready, seek the blade and the control that you desire. It will be your talisman, imbuing you with control. You need only be near the blade for it to work."

"But what if someone steals it?"

"It will always be yours. You can call it back to you."

That was handy. "Who are the Shadows who cursed me?"

"That, I do not know. But you will face them in a great battle. To win, you must embrace your power. Acquire new ones."

Ah, shit. Those were answers I didn't like hearing. "When is this battle?"

She shrugged. The two behind her shrugged as well. Great.

"Am I immortal?" The question had been bugging me ever since I'd come back from the Underworld.

"No. Yes."

"Which is it?" I wanted to add a *damn it*, but bit my tongue. Didn't want to disrespect the Phantom dragon and all.

"All supernaturals are immortal in the sense that there is life after death in the Underworld. You, however, can cross the boundary from the Underworld to Earth, unlike your fellow supernaturals." She peered around me, her gaze pinned to Roarke. "Except for that one. He shares the same power."

"Oh shit. He's not my brother, is he?" I didn't want some Luke Skywalker/Princess Leia situation to go down. I really liked Roarke.

She shook her head. "No. I do not know how he shares that gift. It is rare for all but demons."

Ah, bingo. Because he was half demon, which the Phantoms apparently couldn't sense.

"But to answer your question," she said. "You are immortal in that sense. Though as you've experienced, it's not easy to escape the Underworld."

"Sure isn't." More questions popped to mind. "What about my parents? Who are—"

A great shattering noise exploded through the cavern, then the thunder of footsteps.

Oh no. My ice wall had broken. The Coblynau were coming.

The Phantom's startled gaze met mine. "You didn't kill one, did you?"

"Uh, yeah."

"Stupid! Now they will come for you!"

"I thought they were your protectors! Can't you call them off?"

"No. Not once you have killed one. You must run."

I whirled. A horde of Coblynau had spilled into the cavern. Roarke was out of the water, facing them, ready to battle.

"No time," the Phantom said. Blue light swirled around her as she resumed her dragon form. She leapt into the air, picking me up in one of her massive claws.

Magic surged through me, power like I'd never felt. Almost as if I were hooked up to a magical battery. She replenished all that I had lost, and then some.

She swooped over the lake and plucked up Roarke in her other claw, then clutched us close to her belly.

Roarke's wide gaze met mine as the dragon flew over the horde of goblins and out through the tunnel. I gripped the sword hilt tight in my hand.

Holy fates, this was wild!

As soon as we burst out into the fading sunlight, the cold hit me. I was in my underwear. In the mountains of North Wales. Shivers wracked me as the dragon flew us toward the edge and dropped us into the old iron mining cart. I was jammed in next to Roarke, the cold metal freezing my butt and the sword hilt gripped in my hand.

Behind us, the Coblynau spilled from the mouth of the cave, a maddened horde.

"Use your gift! Bring it to life!" The Phantom dragon's voice sounded in my head.

I looked up, frantic. She hovered in the air above us, her gaze intent on mine.

The Coblynau were nearly upon us. There was no way to outrun them. Especially in my underwear and with Roarke's wings torn up.

"Your gift!"

Shock hit me in the gut when I figured out what she wanted us to do.

She'd fueled up my magic, so it was possible. I gripped the sword hilt tight and called upon my gift over the past, envisioning this place up and running.

In a flash, it burst to life. I didn't even have to struggle for it. The broken-down track repaired itself, and the rust flaked off of the cart. Real miners—not Coblynau—appeared around us, shocked.

The dragon swooped down and nudged our cart with her nose, sending us flying down the ramp. Icy wind burned my eyes as we hurtled down. The enraged screams of the Coblynau sounded from behind us.

"Holy fates!" I cried.

We plowed through the mist, the cart hitting the flat section of the mountain with a bump and careening around the curve, following the track. Another curve and we were on the next ramp, speeding down and out of the mist that had cloaked the mountaintop. An enormous vista of the black quarry and distant mountains stretched out ahead of us.

It was so thrilling that I couldn't even feel the cold, a crazy rollercoaster ride straight out of history. Roarke gripped me from behind, trying to keep me from flying out of the cart. We were hurtling through space as we careened down the mountain. We passed the slate-cutting buildings and the shocked miners, but I had eyes only for the track ahead.

There was another cart, and it wasn't moving nearly as fast as ours since a dragon hadn't given it a nudge.

I focused my magic, imagining that specific cart sent back in time to where it belonged.

It disappeared, easy as that.

I gripped the sword hilt, grateful of its help, and held on for dear life as we plunged down.

When we reached the bottom near the lake, the cart flew off the tracks and skidded onto the beach.

The old boat still sat there, beached just as we'd left it.

Laughing, I turned to Roarke. "Wasn't that amaz— shit! Run!"

Coblynau had caught up. We leapt out of the cart and raced across the beach.

"Morwena!" I screamed. "Help!"

She popped out of the water, her gaze wide, then swam for the boat. We jumped on board just as she climbed up.

"You're going to owe me," she said.

"Okay! Anything!"

Roarke pushed us offshore just as the Coblynau reached the water. Morwena took over from there, using the power of the water to direct the boat to the other shore.

I stood on deck, panting. "Holy fates, that was wild."

"Beyond wild." Roarke joined me, stripping off his jacket and draping it around my shoulders. He then swooped me off my feet and into his arms. Only once my bare feet were off the freezing deck did I realize how damned cold I was.

"Why are you naked?" Morwena asked.

"Long story." I met her gaze where she stood at the back of the boat. "What do I owe you for helping us?"

"A favor. To be determined at a later date."

"Deal." I really didn't have the energy to deal with it right now. I needed a freaking nap.

Roarke carried me all the way to the car. The whole way, I'd clutched the sword hilt to my chest. It'd been a little awkward when we'd walked through the festival, but the nice woman with the hot cocoa stand had given us a blanket and muttered something about the pixies stealing my clothes. We'd let her run with that theory.

By the time Roarke put me in the passenger seat, I'd warmed up a bit from the ride down the mountain. He walked around the front of the car, pulling his phone out of his pocket and punching in a number.

"We need a house. A nice one. With dinner and a healer," he said as he climbed in and cranked the engine. "Text me an address."

He hung up and pulled onto the road, making an eighty-seven-point turn to head back out of town.

"Who was that?" I fiddled with the heat, setting it to blasting.

"Same demon who got us a car. He's arranging a house. After breaking through the blast house, I don't have the strength to get us through the Underpath. I need to recharge."

"How's he going to find a house at this hour?" It was nearly seven at night according to the car's dash clock.

"Holiday homes. You book them on the internet." He glanced at me. "What, did you think we'd stay at his place?"

"No, I uh, didn't think about it much at all. How can you get a house with so little notice?"

"Money."

"So the demons are your travel agents and bankers and healers?"

"And chefs and drivers and messengers and whatever else you can think of."

"Must be nice to be you."

"It's all right." He smiled at me. His phone buzzed and he checked it, then punched an address into the GPS. The destination came up as a place about twenty minutes away. "How are you feeling? That was...an adventure."

"Wasn't it?" I laughed. "I've been on some crazy jobs with Cass and Nix, but this topped all of those!"

"Mercenary jobs?"

I stopped laughing.

Right.

Now was the moment of truth. Should I trust him and fess up? He'd had my back through that whole thing at the mountain and all the time before.

Yeah. I should trust him.

"No." I turned in the seat to look at him. "I'm not just a mercenary. And Ancient Magic isn't just a normal shop."

"I could have guessed that."

"It's how we stock it that's not normal." My heart started to pound. Cass and Nix were okay with this. They *were*. Even Nix, the most suspicious person I'd ever met. I could do this. "I'm not a seeker, like I told you. We're FireSouls. We use our dragon sense to find the treasure."

The car slowed briefly. His hands tightened on the steering wheel, knuckles whitening, and he turned to look at me. "Are you serious?"

"Yeah. But we don't steal powers intentionally. I swear." I swallowed hard, praying he'd believe me.

"Is that how you got the Ubilaz demon's power, though?"

"No. When a FireSoul takes a power, it's a conscious decision. I didn't even realize I was taking the Ubilaz demon's power. I never would have taken that!"

"You would have if you wanted a demon army."

Holy fates. "I don't want one of those."

"I know."

"And it's not like I could control one, even if I had it. You've noticed, right, that they try to kill me? I swear, I didn't do it on purpose. And we're not bad people because we're FireSouls."

"I know that." He glanced at me for a moment, holding my gaze. "You're the best people I've ever met. I like you, Del. And I like your sisters. I'm not going to judge you for what you are. People don't trust me because I'm half demon. I wouldn't do that to you."

He glanced back at the road. I flushed, remembering that I'd held that prejudice about him when I'd first met him.

189

"Thank you for telling me," he said.

My shoulders relaxed. "You won't turn us in?"

But I already knew the answer.

He scowled. "Of course not. But I can understand now why you might have been hesitant to tell me that. And why it seemed that you were hiding something. It's your whole life."

"Exactly. And I've been hiding it a long time. That's a hard switch to turn off. It's ingrained in me." I adopted Gollum's voice and hissed, "Keep it secret, keep it safe."

He laughed as he slowed the car and turned onto a narrow drive.

"Are we here?" I asked.

"Just about."

A moment later, a house appeared at the end of the drive. It was large and old, but very pretty. Just the kind of thing a family would want on holiday.

Two demons came out onto the porch as we pulled up—the one who'd dropped off the car and a plump, grandmotherly-looking one who wore a flowered apron and had small pink horns.

She was *so* different than the demons who were attracted to the Ubilaz's power. She looked really nice, actually.

Roarke stopped the car in front of the steps and came around to my side, pulling me out of the seat as soon as I'd opened the door. He lifted me up against his chest as I clutched the sword hilt that the Phantom dragon had given me.

"You don't have to do that," I said.

He glanced at my feet. "No shoes, remember?"

Now that he'd pointed it out, my toes were cold. And the icy ground looked even colder. As a matter of fact, all I wanted to do right now was thaw my toes in a warm bath.

"You look dreadful," the grandmotherly demon said as we approached.

I frowned.

"Not you, deary." She clucked. "Him."

I glanced up at Roarke, who did look pretty bad. His hair was matted with blood from his head wound, and his face was still pale.

"Thanks," Roarke said. "Are you the healer?"

"Riorda, at your service." She smiled. "And the cook."

"Thank you for coming." He turned to the male demon. "And thank you for setting this up, Florus."

Florus and Riorda nodded, then turned and went into the house. We followed, Roarke carrying me into the lovely old foyer. The wood was warm and gleaming, and the light sparkled from a crystal chandelier.

"You can take a bath if you like," Roarke said as he set me down. "I'm going to let the healer take care of my wings, then we can eat."

"Sounds genius. Thanks." I started up the stairs, which were carpeted in a soft crimson runner that felt divine under my toes. Near the top, I felt the surge of Roarke's magic as he shifted to his demon form. I turned, taking a peek, and winced at the sight of his torn-up wings.

Damn, they looked bad. I hoped the healer could get them back to normal. He didn't deserve that for helping me.

I found a pretty bedroom at the top of the stairs and went inside. It was a large space, done up in many shades of blue, with a four-poster bed and picture windows. Two big armchairs sat in front of a massive fireplace, and a door on the other side gave a glimpse of the bathroom.

I hurried toward my destination, avoiding the mirrors like the plague. No way I looked even halfway decent after what I'd just been through. The sight of the massive, claw footed tub made me grin. It sat at the back of the large bathroom, which was done entirely in cream marble. Whoever had renovated the space had tried to retain the charm and details of the old house, but had given it all of the modern conveniences.

Fancy, fancy.

I set the sword hilt on the ground near the tub and fiddled with the taps, letting the water flow. I stripped off Roarke's coat and my underwear and jumped in as soon as the water was a few inches deep. It was too hot, but I didn't care. Slowly, the tub filled, thawing my muscles.

I stared at the ceiling, replaying the meeting with the Phantom dragons. Curious, I picked up the sword hilt that I'd set on the ground and studied it. The metal was something unique. At one glance, it looked like silver. At another, it looked like gold.

And the carvings... They were so ornate, and their swirls and loops looked almost like words.

The thing felt natural in my hands, and even my chest felt calmer. It was a strange feeling. Almost like my magic felt more tranquil. As if it weren't ricocheting around inside of me, waiting for me to get a handle on it. I still had to find the blade if I wanted to control my Ubilaz power, but I was getting closer.

I could feel it.

I was definitely getting closer with Roarke, too. I was going to get answers to my questions tonight, I hoped. Though I was a bit nervous about it, I felt so much better after laying it all out there.

But what would he reveal? The bombshell about his magic being stronger when he touched me was crazy. Like we were a weird, deathly pair or something.

I shook the thought away. It was more than I wanted to process right now.

Once the water went cold, I climbed out. There were fluffy white towels on the vanity and an even fluffier robe hanging from the hook on the door. I dried off and put on the robe, then picked up the sword hilt, unwilling to let it go from my side. By the time I got out to the bedroom, I was seriously dragging.

The last few days had been exhausting.

The cozy armchairs by the fire called to me. Just one little sit. For a moment.

I sank into the one nearest the window, sighing at how amazing it felt.

Though it was a little chilly, the idea of getting up to build a fire in the hearth was out of the question. Even getting up to hunt down the thermostat wasn't going to happen.

I snuggled deeper into my robe and fiddled with the sword hilt, gazing at the dead hearth.

This fireplace had once had a fire in it. What if I just brought it back?

I gripped the sword hilt and called on my magic. Before I'd even fully envisioned the fireplace roaring with orange flame, it had flickered to life.

Well, that was easy.

The warmth was lovely, glowing and bright. I could even feel that part of my magic inside of me like a distinct part of myself. It glowed like a bright light. As for the Ubilaz demon's power, I could feel that too. It felt cold and dark, sitting right behind my ribcage on the lower left side. And I couldn't control it. Not like I could control my gift over the past.

The thought bummed me out.

I wallowed for a moment, then became annoyed.

I had so much more control than I'd had before! After a good night's sleep, I would find the blade to this sword, and everything would be fine.

To prove that I was getting better with my magic, I tried turning back the clock to a time when a cat might have been in this room. After a moment, a chubby tabby appeared, sleeping on a cushion in front of the fire.

I grinned and sat up straight, making kissy noises.

The cat looked up, and after a brief moment of confusion, stood and stretched, then jumped into my lap. I pet its warm fur, immediately comforted by the little body.

"Maybe I should keep you," I said. "Name you Fang, or something."

The cat just purred.

But of course I couldn't keep him. If I didn't send him back to the past where he belonged, I'd be catnapping him from whatever family he lived with. He clearly had a good life.

I sighed as a knock sounded on the door.

"You better go home," I whispered to the cat, then sent him back to whatever year he'd come from. The cushion disappeared from in front of the fire as well.

The knock sounded again.

"Yes?" I said.

"Can I come in?" Roarke asked.

"Sure."

The door opened and he entered, carrying a tray laden with sandwiches and a box of red wine. He looked much better—clean and healed.

"My favorite," I said. "Thanks."

"I thought you might be too tired to come downstairs." He sat in the chair next to me and handed me a plate. "Cheese and onion."

My stomach growled. "How are you? Are your wings healed?"

"Yes. Riorda is talented." He bit into his sandwich, so I did the same, finally satisfying my growling stomach.

We ate in comfortable silence, starving after our adventures. The cheese and onion sandwiches were excellent, though they sounded like a slightly odd combo.

After Roarke polished off the last of three sandwiches in record time, he poured two mugs of wine and handed one over.

I accepted it gratefully, sipping in delight.

"I suppose I owe you some answers." His tone was uncomfortable but determined.

"That'd be nice," I said.

"And you want to know about my brother."

"That was something I was particularly interested in. But also why you've been so damned distant the last few days. After I killed the Ubilaz demon last week, you said you liked me and you kissed me. Then...nothing. Radio silence. But you never left my side."

He scrubbed a hand through his hair and gazed into the fire. "They're related, in a way."

"Yeah?"

"Yeah." He sat back and met my eyes. "My brother and I didn't know our parents. For a long time, I didn't even know that he existed. We had a couple good years before I figured out anything was wrong. But Caden was involved in dark magic. Really dark."

I winced. That wasn't good.

"I tried to cover it up, thinking that it couldn't possibly be my brother who was doing such terrible things."

"What kind of things?"

"Blood magic. The deadly kind. Not just the unwilling, steal-your-memory kind that was performed on Orson Reyes. But the kind that takes all of the victim's blood to perform a terrible ritual."

I swallowed hard. "Shit."

"Yeah. And it turned out that it was him performing the rituals. If I'd stopped him sooner—if I'd just followed the standards and the morals that I held everyone else to—he wouldn't have killed so many people." He shook his head, his pained gaze somewhere far in the past. "I don't even know what kind of magic he was trying to perform. Only that half a dozen people died because I didn't follow my own rules."

"But he was your brother. You were trying to protect him."

"It doesn't make it right. I tried to get Horatio from Cambridge to help, but he could do nothing. By the time I handed my brother over to people who could control him, it was too late. Too many people had died." He met my gaze. "So you can understand why I might have been reticent to share this."

"Yeah. But you tried your best."

A sad smile tugged at the corner of his mouth. "That doesn't really help in this circumstance. I still failed."

I could understand that. Hating that you failed even though you'd tried your best. "So what does this have to do with being so weird around me?"

"I don't want to fuck up with you the way I fucked up with my brother—not that I believe I'll need to turn you in for something. But my love for my brother blinded me. I didn't see warning signs because I was too preoccupied."

He took a sip of wine and I waited, knowing he wasn't done yet. "I was alone a long time before Caden and I found each other. It's not easy for half-bloods to make friends, so I spent a lot of time on my own. But there was a benefit. I mastered my powers. Became good at my work. I was focused, compartmentalized. But emotion—even just love for my brother—that distracted me. I made mistakes." His pained gaze met mine. "I don't want to make mistakes with you. I need to protect you."

My heart twisted. "I can protect myself."

"I know you can. It's one of the things I like about you. But whatever is coming for you—whatever you are supposed to guard against—that may be more than one person can handle. Hell, it probably is. So I tried to compartmentalize again. Focus just on the goal—helping you learn your magic and survive whatever is coming. I didn't want to make the same mistake twice."

My heart thumped in my chest, painfully hard. Any doubts I'd ever had about him fled in that moment. I set my mug on the floor, then rose and went to him, sitting in his lap.

He looped his arms around my waist, and the sense of rightness that I felt was comparable only to when I was with my *deirfiúr*.

"Why do you think your magic is stronger when you touch me?" I asked.

"I don't know. I wish I did. It's easier to break through to the Underpath when I hold your hand. That's how I realized it. At first I thought it was coincidence, but then I realized it was you. It's one of the smaller reasons I've been…distant, I guess you'd say. I was trying to figure it out. You're special somehow. Your magic. You."

Yeah, but how? I wish I knew.

"But we're starting a new chapter," he said. "Total honesty."

I smiled. "You're a good guy, Roarke Fallon."

He met my gaze. "Not sure about that. But I try."

"I know." I leaned in and kissed him, pressing my lips to his. This time, he didn't pull way. Instead, he sank deeper into the kiss, clutching the back of my head as his lips moved expertly on mine.

I sank my hands into his soft hair. His lips felt divine, soft and warm and so skilled that the kiss stole all my thoughts. I was floating in a dream world that smelled, tasted, and felt like Roarke. I never wanted to leave.

After a moment, he pulled away.

"We need to rest," he said. "As much as I'd like to take this farther, I've called Cass and Nix, and they'll be here soon."

I tried to catch my breath. "You did?"

"Yes. It's vital that we get the blade to your sword, and they may be able to help. I thought you would want them here."

"I do." He was right about that. And he was also right about the fact that I needed to rest. The day was finally catching up with me, and my muscles felt like lead.

"Okay," I said. "Let's take a nap. Together."

He grinned, so sexy that my blood heated despite the exhaustion.

"I could be okay with that," he said.

"Good. Me too."

He stood, carrying me to the bed, and yanked back the covers before putting me in the middle. He then climbed in after me, tucking me in against his side. I curled into him, exhaustion pulling me deep.

CHAPTER TWELVE

"Wake up!" Cass's voice carried down the hall.

Blearily, I opened my eyes. Roarke was gone, which was probably for the best, because Cass and Nix burst into the room a moment later.

"So, you worked it out with Roarke!" Cass cried as she hurtled into the room.

I sat up and shoved my hair off my face, yawning. "How could you tell?"

"Every other bed in this house is already made," Nix said. "Come on, dude, we're problem solvers. Of course we noticed."

"Nothing happened," I said.

"Not *yet*." Cass wiggled her eyebrows.

I threw a pillow at her.

"Oof." She doubled over, clutching the pillow to her middle.

"But thank you for coming." I climbed out of bed and straightened my fluffy robe. "Any chance you brought me some clean clothes?"

"You know it." Nix tossed a duffle bag on the bed. "And another sword and sheath from Cass's collection. Roarke said you might need it."

"You're a hero." I changed quickly while Cass and Nix explored the room.

"This place is nice," Cass said.

"Yeah." I strapped the new sword sheath to my back and picked up the hilt of the sword that the Phantom dragon had given me.

"You've got some answers?" Nix asked as she came out of the bathroom.

"Yeah. Let's go down and get something to eat, and we can talk about it." I was famished, and from the pale gray light coming in the window, it looked like it was dawn. Breakfast time.

We found Roarke and Aidan in the kitchen. Aidan leaned against the wall, drinking a cup of coffee, while Roarke poked at a massive skillet of eggs. It was an older, homier room, with a black slate floor and little framed pictures all over the walls, and the men looked distinctly out of place. Too big and too deadly looking, despite the spatula in Roarke's hand.

Roarke and I traded smiles, then I looked at Aidan.

"Aidan! You came," I said.

"'Course." He nodded at Roarke. "Just chatting with your friend here. It sounds like you have an adventure ahead of you. And behind you."

"Adventure." I thought of the dragons and the crazy ride down the mountain in the mining cart. "Yeah, adventure just about covers it."

Roarke filled two platters with bacon and eggs, then nodded at the table. "Food's up."

"Thanks." I grabbed a cup of coffee from the pot. I kept the sword hilt near me at all times, putting it in my lap as we all sat at the round table in the corner of the kitchen.

We dished up plates. As the first bite of eggs was headed to my mouth, Cass asked, "So what are we up against? Why are you carrying around a broken sword hilt?"

I set down the fork and pulled the sword hilt off my lap. "This is half of a talisman that will help me control the Cat 5 powers."

"The Ubilaz demon powers," Nix said.

"Exactly." Between bites of eggs, I filled them in on what the Phantom dragon had told me—about how I'd have to use my dragon sense to find the blade and prove myself worthy of obtaining it.

"That's not so hard," Cass said.

I swallowed my last bite. "No, not normally. But I still have demons after me. Though I've finally got control of my other magic."

"Well, that's something," Nix said. "When do you want to get started?"

"I'm thinking right about now."

"Sounds good," Aidan said.

"Since Roarke was good enough to cook, we'll clean up," Cass said. "You, Del, can figure out where we're going to get this blade."

"You're coming?" Even as I asked the question, I knew the answer.

"Duh," Cass said. "You might need help. I'm sick of sitting around and letting you do this alone. And anyway, I want to be there to claim some credit."

I grinned. "Thanks."

They cleaned up the dishes while I stayed in my chair, closing my eyes and focusing on my dragon sense. It was a little weird to use it around Roarke even though he knew exactly what I was doing, but it was fine.

When my dragon sense finally caught on and tugged, my eyes popped open. "Oh crap."

"What is it?" Roarke demanded, coming to stand in front of me.

"My dragon sense wants me to go through the portal near your house. To the Underworld."

"Damn it." Roarke rubbed his forehead.

"Lots of demons in there, I bet." Cass threw the dishtowel she'd been using on the counter. "Sounds like it will be a fight."

"As long as we stick to my part of the Underworld, no," Roarke said. "I have jurisdiction there. The demons will follow my command and not attack. But if we have to take a portal to another Underworld, then we're in trouble. I rule those places through command over their king, not the subjects themselves. So if we happen to meet any wayward demons, they won't necessarily listen to me."

"And they'll attack," Nix said.

I looked at Roarke. "Is it even possible for them to go to the Underworld without dying?"

He nodded. "If I escort them through personally, then yes. But they won't be able to get out unless I accompany them."

"So if you get killed while we're there, we're stuck?" Nix asked.

"Yes," Roarke said. "And if *you* get killed there, then you're stuck."

I grimaced.

"Then we'll just have to make sure none of us get offed," Cass said.

I met her gaze. "Are you sure you want to do this?"

"Wouldn't miss it." Her voice was firm. "And you're going to need the help if you want any chance of making it to your sword. If we have to leave Roarke's area, demons will be on you like white on rice, and you're going to need help fighting them off."

She was right. "Thank you."

"But once you're in your Underworld, how do we get to other ones?" Nix asked.

"More portals," Roarke said. "They're scattered over the different Underworld realms, connecting each of them."

"So we just have to go and see where my dragon sense leads, then," I said.

Roarke nodded.

I stood, nerves making my skin feel extra sensitive. "We might as well get a move on."

"I can transport us to Roarke's house," Cass said. "It'll save time."

"Thank you." It still kinda stung not to have my transportation power—I'd used it for so long it had become part of me—but Cass was always good about giving me a ride. And I had plenty of powers now. Too many, in fact.

Everyone made quick work of getting their things together. I strapped the sword hilt into the sheath that Nix had brought and carried the actual sword in my hand, ready to be used if necessary.

When we were all ready, we gathered around Cass. Because of her massive amount of magical power, she was able to transport many people at once.

"Okay, children," she said in a singsong voice. "Everyone stand in a circle and hold hands."

I grinned and grabbed Roarke's and Nix's hands.

Once we were all connected, Cass smiled and said, "Here we go."

The ether sucked us in, a whirlwind ride that spit us out in the woods near Roarke's house. At least, I thought it was near Roarke's house. It was dark, the sliver of moon shedding hardly any light at all.

"Where's the house?" Nix asked.

"Eh, somewhere nearby?" Cass said. "I've never actually been here, so I was guessing based upon what Del had told me before."

"It's okay." I used my dragon sense to find the portal. "The portal is only about a hundred yards away."

We set off through the woods, eventually coming upon the portal. It had been repaired since the last time I'd torn through it, so I could feel it but not see it.

"We're here, right?" I asked.

"Yes," Roarke said. He turned to my friends. "I'll have to hold your hands as you go through. You need to be touching me to pass over."

"We'll go first." Cass grabbed Aidan's hand and stepped toward Roarke.

Roarke gripped Cass's and Aidan's hands, and they stepped forward, disappearing into thin air.

"Crazy," Nix said.

"Yeah."

Roarke returned a moment later, grabbing Nix's hand and pulling her through. I adopted my Phantom form and followed, stepping through the portal without a problem.

On the other side, my friends stood in Roarke's garden. I'd forgotten how pretty it was, and how different from the rest of the Underworld. The air smelled of flowers and was slightly damp, as if it'd just rained. Tumbling roses grew on the path on either side, and every shade of green surrounded us.

"This isn't so bad," Cass said as a swan floated by on the lake.

"Wait until you see the rest," I said.

We set off through the garden, encountering only swans and flowers. By the time we reached the house at the other end, I was vibrating with tension, just waiting to stumble into a demon. No matter what Roarke said about being able to control the demons here, I did *not* want to run into one.

Even being here at all made me feel like I might have to stay.

Roarke led the way into the main foyer. I'd been out of my mind with fear and pain last time I'd been here, running for my life, so I hadn't been able to fully appreciate the grandeur of the massive space. In all fairness, I probably wasn't appreciating it now, with my eyes darting all over the place looking for demons.

"Whew." Nix whistled as she looked up at the high ceiling. "This place is fancy."

"It's really more for show," Roarke said. "Demons respect strength and wealth."

"Who doesn't?" I asked.

As soon as the words were out of my mouth, four hulking demons walked into the hall. They were dark gray with massive horns. Dozens of weapons were clipped to their leather utility vests like horrible ornaments.

The deadly Christmas trees. I remembered these jerks. They'd chased me down last time I was here.

Unable to help myself, I stiffened.

Their gazes were drawn immediately to me, making my heart race, but they didn't linger. Instead, they lowered their eyes and knelt before Roarke.

"Warden," they rumbled in unison.

"Rise," Roarke said.

They rose, their gazes on him. They were scary bastards, but not as scary as Roarke. His demeanor had changed, and though he technically looked no different, something in his eyes and posture made it clear that he was the boss.

"We need a guard," he said. "You will escort us. There is a chance that we may depart for another

Underworld. In that case, you will attack any other demon that approaches us."

They nodded in unison, then took up position behind us.

"Lead on," Roarke said to me.

I focused on my dragon sense, picking up the thread of direction and following it out the front door and into the courtyard. It was grayer and darker here, nothing like the beautiful garden out back. But by the time we reached the gate and walked over the drawbridge that spanned the smelly moat, it was clear we were in hell.

"I see what you mean," Cass muttered.

"Right?" The horrible vista stretched out before me, a barren hellscape punctuated by patches of flame and an endless expanse of jagged black rocks. A strange gray haze shimmered on the air.

"I can see why you choose to live in Magic's Bend," Nix said to Roarke.

"Commuting is better," he agreed.

Our demon guard tromped along behind us as we made our way over the jagged rocks, dodging the crevasses that plunged deep into the ground. Sweat rolled down my skin as we walked. Though we encountered demons, they took one look at Roarke and hurried about their business.

We'd been walking for over an hour by the time we reached a portal. It was a shimmering black hole in the air, unlike the one on Earth. Here in the Underworld, they weren't concerned with hiding portals from humans.

My dragon sense pulled inexorably toward it. I'd been expecting it—no way this was going to be so easy that I found the sword blade in Roarke's Underworld—but it made my heart race all the same.

"We have to go through," I said.

"I'm not sure where this one leads." Roarke turned toward the demons and pointed to the two nearest to him. "Morphus and Kartis, come with me. We'll check it out first."

The two demons nodded and stepped forward. Roarke didn't have to take their hands as they stepped through. All three disappeared.

The Underworld suddenly felt different without Roarke. *Way* more threatening. I glanced back at the other two demons, whose gazes were riveted to me. Confusion and something like anger or annoyance glittered in their black eyes.

Great. Just the kind of enemy I wanted.

A moment later, two figures hurtled out of the portal, straight at us. I stumbled back as Roarke tossed onto the ground the frozen blue body of one of the demons who'd accompanied him. He ducked back into the portal and returned with one more frozen demon, throwing him onto the ground next to the first. They looked like cartoons of mountaineers who'd been trapped on a snowy mountain.

"We have a problem," he said.

At my feet, the demons began to lose their blue tinge as they thawed.

"Are they dead?" I asked. "What's over there? Mount Everest?"

"Basically," Roarke said. "It's an ice hell. Morphus and Kartis aren't dead, but they're close. Their species can't survive the cold, not like human bodies can."

They must be native to this sweltering hellscape.

"That means we're losing our guards," Aidan said.

"Yes."

Roarke turned to the two demons who were still standing. "See that your colleagues are revived. Thank you for accompanying us. You may resume your normal duties."

The two demons bowed low, then each hauled up the body of one of the others. After tossing them over their shoulders, they turned and headed back across the fiery wasteland of Roarke's Underworld.

"On our own." Nix rubbed her hands together. "We've got this."

I sure hoped so.

We went through the portal the same way we'd passed through the other—in groups.

As soon as I stepped out on the other side, I sucked in a harsh breath, then coughed. The air was so cold it felt like my lungs were frozen.

Ahead of me stretched the most awe-inspiring vista I'd ever seen. It was like we were on top of Everest, but we were surrounded by a hundred more Everests. Jagged mountains coated with snow stretched as far as the eye could see. The wind whipped at fifty miles an hour—or something crazy strong like that; I wasn't a meteorologist—blowing my hair back off my face and making my eyes water.

"This sucks!" I yelled over the wind.

"Can I transport us to the end goal?" Cass asked.

Roarke shook his head. "Safer to walk. That way we know what we're heading into. We could appear in the middle of a mass of demons, otherwise."

He had a point. I shivered hard as I called upon my dragon sense. The tug came quickly. "We're not far!"

"Lead the way," Roarke shouted over the wind.

We tromped through the snow, heading downward in a single-file line. I was freezing, but the exertion kept me from going entirely numb. At one point, my feet slipped out from under me, but Roarke grabbed me before I could hurtle down the mountainside.

"Thanks!" I kept going.

A few moments later, we came upon another portal.

"Please lead us somewhere warm," I muttered.

"I'll check it out first," Roarke said.

"I'll come with."

He nodded and we stepped through to a dark forest. Tall black-trunked trees loomed overhead, the size of redwoods. Forest creatures rustled in the distance, but I saw nothing that would kill us immediately.

"Looks fine," Roarke said. "I'll go get the others."

Roarke returned with Aidan, Cass, and Nix a moment later, making two trips while I scouted out the nearby area.

It almost felt familiar, but it was such a vague sensation that it was impossible to place. I definitely didn't recognize it. The trees weren't even a type that could possibly occur on Earth. But the sword blade had to be near. I could feel it.

"I think we're close." I set off between the trees, my friends following.

Ahead, something dark flickered, but it disappeared as soon as I saw it. My dragon sense pulled me toward it.

We'd only made it a few yards when something crashed out of the forest. A large, pale demon, its eyes wild, hurtled toward us. Another crashed through the forest behind it.

The rustling in the distance hadn't been forest creatures—it'd been demons. My heart thundered. I gripped the sword tight.

More appeared, drawn by my Ubilaz power. Their eyes riveted to me, confusion and then anger showing on their faces.

"Yeah, yeah. I stole your buddy's power," I muttered.

Beside me, a tornado of black mist swirled around Roarke. Golden light shone from Aidan. They transformed at the same time—a dark gray winged demon standing next to a golden griffin. They took off into the air, charging the demons.

More ran out from between the trees, all different species. There must have been a town nearby or something.

Cass raced forward, throwing a fireball as she ran. It lit up the nearest demon. Nix's magic surged on the air as she conjured a bow. She fired into the horde while Roarke dipped low, grabbing them up and snapping their necks.

I didn't want to use my borrowed sword for fear of taking the demons' powers, so I plunged it into the ground where I could retrieve it if I really needed it. With a deep breath, I called upon my ice power and shot a thick icicle at the nearest demon. It pierced his chest and bowled him over. I spun and attacked another, dodging as one leapt for me. Cass hit him with a fireball, and he stumbled away, ablaze.

"Thanks!" I called.

Magic blasted through the air, followed by the screams of demons, as I searched the forest. I could feel the sword blade. It was so close—my dragon sense shouted it.

In the distance, the air flashed silver. A portal. It had to be. The one that held the sword.

I raced for it, crying out to Roarke as I passed, "We're close! It's in that portal up ahead."

"We'll follow!" Roarke yelled. "I'll bring the others!"

I left him behind and sprinted the last ten yards, dodging a demon's fireball as I ran. A shadow flickered through the portal, leading me to it. A sense of rightness filled me as I neared it—I was close to the blade.

I could hear my friends running behind me, crashing through the forest to get to the next portal. I adopted my Phantom form right before I reached it, plunging inside.

CHAPTER THIRTEEN

I skidded to a halt on the other side, my eyes widening. I was back in the tower. The one from my childhood. In my mind, I was immediately in the past, as if my present self were joined with my younger self. My head buzzed with the combination of adult knowledge and childish yearning.

Being here made me want to see my parents *so badly*. Even though my only memories were of their abandonment, I couldn't help but think that if I just saw them, everything would be okay. And I would have answers.

I knew it like I knew I needed air to breathe.

I spun, taking in the empty room. Or was it empty? I almost felt a presence, but I wasn't sure. Draka, maybe?

Behind me, the portal glowed like a window into the forest I'd just left behind. My friends ran toward me— toward the portal.

Roarke grabbed Cass's and Nix's hands and stepped forward.

He pulled up short, as if he had hit a wall. Confusion flashed over his face. He tried again, but he couldn't get through.

I could see Cass's lips move, but I couldn't hear her. She wanted to know what was wrong. From behind my friends, more demons appeared, running out from between the trees. An endless supply of them. Aidan, still in his griffin form, roared to warn them. They all turned. Cass threw a fireball at the nearest demon while Nix fired her arrows.

As my friends defended themselves, I turned back to the room, unable to help myself. My mind buzzed with memories, all elusive as smoke. I couldn't quite grasp them, but they were here. The blade was here.

Somewhere.

But I couldn't feel where.

The door on the other side of the room was open.

The exit!

My heart leapt. It'd never been open before—not while I was unsupervised. I could run down and see my parents.

Vaguely, I recognized that my mind had gone back to the past. Back to when I was a girl, locked up here until I learned to fight and use my magic.

Do what is right. Draka's words from my dream echoed in my head.

My gaze stayed riveted on the door. I could just run down. I *should* just run down. I would see my parents. I would have a good life with my family. The life I once wanted, beautiful and pure. I wouldn't end up with the Ubilaz demon's power.

Even better, I'd have answers about my past.

And the sword blade had to be down there. Why else would I have come here?

But what about my friends?

I turned, gazing out of the portal at the people I'd grown to love like my own blood. More demons had arrived. They fought valiantly, Roarke and Aidan swooping through the air and diving for the demons' heads while Cass and Nix shot fire and arrows.

But there were so many demons.

I turned away, gazing at the room once more. My heart ached like it had never ached before, pulling me toward the open door. Would I find Draka down there? My parents?

Yes.

My parents, yes.

But I knew, like I knew my own soul, that if I went down those stairs, I would never come back up. I might find the life I'd wished for, but I'd never see my *deirfiúr* again. Never see Roarke again.

But the sword was here, somewhere in this world. I could feel it.

Unable to help myself, I turned back to the portal to see my friends.

More demons had arrived. They wouldn't stop arriving. Roarke and Aidan could fly out of there, taking Cass and Nix with them. But they wouldn't leave without me. They'd die fighting for me.

My chest hurt.

They needed me. I couldn't stay here. Not even for the sword blade.

There was no time to search for it. Not as long as the demons kept piling up on my friends, flowing out of the forest like a wave of evil.

My heart tore in two. If I left here, I'd be leaving the sword blade behind. Leaving behind any hope of controlling the last of my power—the worst of my power. It would be the death of me, sooner rather than later. I'd leave behind any hope of knowing my family.

But if I stayed, I'd leave my friends to die.

Do what is right. Draka's words echoed in my head as I stepped toward the portal. I had to fight by their side. I had to be there so they would escape—not stay here and let them die, trying to defend a friend who had abandoned them.

As I stepped toward the portal, the sword sheath at my back twitched. I was about to reach for it when something grabbed me from behind and yanked me back into the room.

For the first time since I'd entered the tower, my mind cleared fully. I slammed onto my back on the floor. A black shadow swirled above me, amorphous but vaguely shaped like a cloaked man.

Shit!

The shadow that had cursed me?

My head ached, as if the curse in my mind were reacting to its nearness.

Yes. The shadow that had cursed me.

I threw out my hand, calling on my ice power, and sent a massive icicle straight at it. The spear flew through the shadow and shattered against the ceiling, raining icy shards down upon me. I rolled, protecting my face, but the shadow jerked me up.

I thrashed, trying to break its hold, but it was so strong! Fear chilled my skin, and I wished desperately for help. Any kind of help.

A dog's bark sounded, so familiar and beautiful. Pond Flower hurtled from the other side of the room, black flame rising from her skin and her teeth bared. She leapt through the shadow, driving it away from me.

I whirled to face it just as it surged back toward me. I hurled another icicle at it. Again, the icicle shot through the shadow.

On the other side of the room, I could see my friends, still fighting. Dozens of demons surrounded them, throwing fire and wind and all manner of magical weapons. Nix was down, struggling to rise. Cass stumbled. Blood poured from Roarke's chest, and Aidan's golden fur was streaked with soot from fireballs.

My heart thundered, panic racing through me. I had to get to them! They were so badly outnumbered.

Something tugged at the sheath on my back. Pond Flower!

Why was she tugging at the sword hilt?

I reached for the sword, pulling so hard that the straps containing it broke.

As I drew the sword in front of me, the shadow spun around to face me. Shock lanced through me at the sight of my sword. From the hilt, a bright blue blade was growing.

My magic screamed inside of me, lighting up like fireworks. I blinked, trying to focus on the black shadow that was surging toward me. I swung out with the blade, aiming for the shadow. When the glowing blue metal swept through its middle, it hissed. I struck again, and this time, smoke rose up from it.

The shadow whirled, racing across the room and disappearing out the door. For the briefest second, I longed to go after it, but I ignored that feeling.

It wasn't gone, but that battle would have to wait for another day.

My magic was going wild inside of me. Like for the first time, I could feel all of it. Identify all of it. Different powers glowed as different lights. As I'd once imagined, the Ubilaz demon's power glowed as a bright orange light.

In my mind, I reached out and grabbed it, getting ahold of it so easily. As easily as if I were turning into a Phantom or throwing an icicle. It was nothing to snuff it out, dampening the power and the call to all the demons that it seemed to emit.

Pond Flower barked with joy.

"Thank you," I told her. She'd come when I'd truly needed her. Apparently she only showed when I was at my most desperate.

I'd take it.

Pond Flower licked my hand once, then disappeared.

Joy sang through me as I raced through the portal, stumbling out into the woods. None of the demons looked at me funny, like I was an abomination they needed to kill.

It had worked!

I joined the battle, testing my new blade against a nearby demon. As it sliced through his neck, instinct made me reject his power. He stumbled back, collapsing, but his soul didn't fly out and cling to me.

"You're back!" Cass cried.

"Yeah!" I plunged my sword into the chest of another demon, this one massive and with huge fangs. With my blade sunk into his chest, I kicked him hard to dislodge him.

Twenty feet away, a small yellow demon crept up on Nix. I shot an icicle at it, nailing it in the stomach.

I liked this new multitasking!

Sweat poured down my face as I fought, but at least new demons had stopped appearing. I was no longer attracting them with my Ubilaz power, thank fates.

Eventually, all the demons lay dead around us. My shoulder burned from a fireball wound and a cut on my leg dripped blood, but I looked better than my friends. Every single one of them was bleeding from multiple wounds and singed with fireball blasts.

Roarke staggered up to me, one of his wings drooping.

"It worked." His gaze went to my sword. He grinned.

"It did."

He gripped the back of my neck and pressed a kiss to my forehead.

"Good job," Cass said. "Whatever you had to do."

"Not ditch my friends," I said.

"What?"

"Long story." I glanced around the woods, looking for more demons. They were no longer drawn to me, but I didn't want to run into one accidentally. We were just about out of fight juice. "Let's get out of here, and I'll tell you."

We tromped off through the woods, following my dragon sense back toward the portal. I held Roarke's hand, while Cass and Nix leaned on each other. Aidan stalked ahead, still in his griffin form.

My heart warmed. I'd made the right choice. No matter how much I'd wanted answers and to meet my family, *this* was my family. The family that I'd chosen. And who had chosen me.

Walking with my friends, victorious after battle, was pretty much the best feeling in the world.

CHAPTER FOURTEEN

The next evening, I pushed open the door to P & P, grateful to duck in out of the rain. It'd been nearly a full twenty-four hours since we'd arrived back on Earth, and I was supposed to meet my friends here for a recap. They'd all been so tired and injured when we'd finally made it back that we'd agreed on a short break so everyone could heal up. After the healer had seen to him, Roarke had spent the night at my place, both of us just relaxing until we passed out from exhaustion, but he'd headed back to his place to change about an hour ago.

I was the first to get to P & P, where we'd all agreed to meet, which was part of my plan.

"Hey!" Claire called from behind the counter. "You're just in time."

"Good." I walked through the empty cafe, pulling the dagger out of the bag at my side. "I've brought the artifact. Will Orson be here soon?"

Claire came around the corner and took the dagger from me. "Yes. I told him I'd found the artifact that had been imbued with the Ubilaz demon's magic and destroyed the magic. He's agreed to come get the dagger."

"Awesome." The true point of inviting Orson to P & P was to see if he recognized me. If the blood spell had worked, he shouldn't. Claire had emptied out the cafe so we'd be alone, just in case his memory hadn't been wiped.

At that point, we'd have to deal with him.

"Have a seat, and I'll bring you a drink." She pointed toward the corner near the bar. Not my usual seat, but it would ensure that Orson saw me when he entered.

I sat, enjoying the fact that I didn't have to shift to make a sword sheath fit comfortably. I'd figured out pretty quickly how to store my new blade in the ether and draw it whenever I needed. It meant that the talisman was always with me, but I didn't need to carry it. And that meant no demons showing up randomly.

I pulled out my phone and began to idly scroll through it, waiting for Orson and trying to look relaxed. In reality, every muscle was tense.

"One mug of red wine." Connor's voice made me jerk my head up.

He grinned at me, holding the mug out in front of his usual obscure band T-shirt. Today, it was Alterbridge. Who the heck was Alterbridge?

"Thanks!" I reached up and took the mug.

He sat in the seat near mine and grinned. "I'll keep you company while we wait. Nervous?"

"Yeah."

"Well, we shouldn't—"

The door opened behind him, cutting him off.

It was Orson, impeccably dressed as usual in a long black raincoat that had clearly been custom made. I stiffened slightly, then forced myself to relax and sip the wine Connor had brought me.

Connor, bless him, began to make inane conversation about Alterbridge while Orson stalked across the coffee shop.

His gaze passed briefly over me, and though it paused, it didn't stick. My heart calmed slightly.

Claire came out of the back kitchen just as he reached the bar.

"Do you have it?" Orson demanded.

"Yes." Claire pulled the dagger from underneath the counter where she'd stashed it and handed it over. "A mage helped me remove the spell. But the Ubilaz demon's powers are gone for good now."

Orson nodded. "Good. I can feel that there are no more disturbances in the demon power sphere. The Order of the Magica will be pleased. I should get a raise for this!"

I suppressed a scowl. If anyone should get a raise, it should be Claire. To her credit, she just nodded and smiled. She was used to her crappy boss.

I held my breath as Orson walked out of the coffee shop. He glanced at me one more time, but there was nothing more than disinterest in his gaze. As soon as he disappeared down the street, Claire came over.

"It worked," she said with a smile.

"Yeah." My shoulders loosened. "Thank fates."

The door opened a moment later, and Cass and Aidan came in. Both looked vastly better than they had after we'd escaped the Underworld. Nix and Roarke followed almost immediately.

"You're all punctual," I said.

"You're early," Cass said.

"I was supposed to be." Guiltily, I fessed up. "Claire and I arranged it so that Orson would come and pick up an artifact that was supposedly imbued with the Ubilaz demon's power. We wanted to see if he recognized me."

Roarke leaned down and kissed me briefly. My heart fluttered as he said, "He didn't, I presume?"

"No. Thank magic."

"Good!" Cass shook her finger. "But you're an idiot for doing that without us!"

"I couldn't let him know you were my accomplices if he *did* recognize me. You guys have already done enough."

"Nah," Nix said. "That little fight in hell was fun!"

"Fun. Right." I grinned at her.

"We're going to get some drinks," Cass said. "Then you can tell us what the hell happened back there."

While Claire got drinks for everyone, Connor hopped up and turned on some music. It was some obscure band I'd never heard of—maybe Alterbridge themselves—but that didn't matter. I was so happy to be with everyone and have everything mostly back to normal that he could have played Gregorian chants and I'd have liked it.

Roarke was the first to join me, settling into the seat next to mine. He leaned over and kissed me briefly, sending my heart rate skyrocketing.

"How're you doing?" he asked.

"Great. My magic feels totally in control. Like my whole body is in harmony." I searched his handsome face, looking for any sign of the bruising he'd had yesterday. Those demons had done a number on everyone. "More importantly, how are you?"

"Good. All healed up."

"Good."

Cass plopped down in the seat next to me, a silver can of her horrible PBR clutched in her hand.

"So, spill," she said.

Aidan sat next to her, and Nix joined us a moment later. Claire and Connor took the last two seats, rounding out our little private party nicely.

"Thanks for closing the cafe for this," I said.

"No problem," Claire said. "It's usually a quiet night anyway. And I didn't want anyone here when Orson came to get the dagger."

"I'm so glad he's off your tail," Nix said. "Now tell us what happened back there."

"Okay." I sucked in a deep breath and told them about the tower room and the shadow. About having to make the right choice to prove I was worthy.

Once I'd finished, Cass asked, "So, you think by choosing us, you did the right thing, and that's what made the sword blade appear?"

"Yeah," I said. "I mean, it was a no-brainer. I'd love to know my parents and get some answers, but your lives were on the line. And you're my family. I really think that if I went down those stairs, that I'd never have come back up. I'd never see you again."

"Maybe that's because of the shadow," Roarke said. "Because if you ask me, that sounds a hell of a lot like a trap."

I nodded, dread twisting my insides. "I think you're right. And I think that shadow was what cursed me. But I didn't kill it. It's still out there."

"But at least now you have control of your powers," Nix said.

"And I'd bet big money you're going to get a second crack at that shadow," Cass added.

"Yeah." I sat back, clutching my wine in both hands. "I just wish I knew what happened to Draka. I'm going to need her help."

"You have our help," Roarke said.

"And ours." Claire grabbed her brother's hand.

He grinned.

"Thanks, guys."

Being surrounded by my friends—my family—was amazing. Having Roarke here made it even better.

I may have just obtained a bunch of crazy new powers, but at least now I could control them. I may not know what was in my past, but I had clues.

Best of all, I felt like I might actually have a shot at handling this Guardian thing. It'd scared me before—and if I was honest, it still scared me—but I could overcome that. With my friends at my back, anything was possible.

THANK YOU FOR READING!

Want to find out how Del died? Dragon's Gift: The Huntress, which stars Cass, is the series to read. There is an excerpt of book one, Ancient Magic, on the next page.

Reviews are so helpful to authors. I really appreciate all reviews, both positive and negative. If you want to leave one, you can do so at Amazon or GoodReads.

Turn the page for an excerpt of Ancient Magic.

PROLOGUE

Blood. I rubbed my tongue against the top of my mouth. Definitely blood. Fear shivered through me. The ground scratched my bare arms and the back of my neck. Prickly grass? My eyelids were gritty as I lifted them and blinked into the darkness. Stars twinkled down.

Night? Where was I?

Panic closed my throat. I gasped for air.

I pushed myself up and looked down. A ragged dress covered my skinny form, but didn't protect me from the chill night. I shivered as cold embraced me. A battered golden locket lay on my chest. It looked old, but I didn't recognize it.

A field stretched out around me, illuminated by starlight and a moon that hung low over the earth. The hair on my arms stood up at the sound of night creatures in the distance. A cold breeze rustled the grass, but fear chilled me more than the wind. Why was I out here?

Please don't let me be alone.

My heart thundered in my ears as I glanced around.

Two girls who looked to be about fourteen or fifteen lay sprawled on the ground beside me. They wore ragged dresses like mine.

Why was I here with two other girls my age?

Wait—were they my age? When I thought about it, I couldn't remember how old I was exactly. Just trying to think of it sent an icepick of pain through my skull.

With a trembling hand, I reached out and shook the girl closest to me.

"Wake up," I said. Panic sunk its claws into my chest. Why were we here?

When she didn't wake, I shouted, "Wake up!"

The girl gasped and shot upright, her black hair stuck with grass. Her terrified blue eyes met mine.

"Run," she gasped.

She spoke Irish, like I did, and the word shot straight through me.

"Hide," I said. "We have to hide."

I wasn't sure why, but I knew it more strongly than I knew anything else in the world. Her word—*run*—had triggered my own. *Hide.*

"Get up!" I scrambled to my feet. "We have to hide. Now. Now, now, now."

She clambered up, and we frantically tugged at the arms of the girl who still lay on her back. She was so pale she looked dead.

But I couldn't leave her. "Get up!"

She shrieked and jerked out of our hold, then crouched like a terrified animal. Her dark hair hung in her face.

What had happened to her, to us, that we were like this?

"FireSoul," she whispered, also in Irish. Her wide green gaze met mine through the curtain of hair.

The fear in her eyes must have mirrored my own. Her word pricked at my consciousness, but fear overrode it.

My heart pounded in my chest, trying to break my ribs. "Come on. We have to hide!"

She nodded and her head whipped around, searching for shelter like a cornered animal. I looked too. A small patch of woods about a hundred yards behind me caught my eye.

"This way." I spun and set off running across the field. They followed.

My lungs burned and my legs ached as we raced. I clearly wasn't used to being outside, nor to exercise.

But why? When I tried to think of the reason, nothing came but pain. My head ached when I tried to remember myself or my past. A sob burst from my chest. I couldn't remember anything.

Fear and the desperate need to hide drove me on when I wanted to stop and collapse to the ground, weeping. The trees loomed ahead—leafless, claw-like branches reaching for the sky. They were terrifying, but far better than the open field.

There was nowhere to hide in an open field.

Hide.

We dove into the woods, plowing through the underbrush until we were deep in the forest. Night creatures continued to rustle around us.

When we came to a large pile of collapsed trees, I plunged into them. Bark and branches scratched my arms as I found a nook created by the collapsed wood. The other girls crowded in behind me.

They were warm. Familiar, though I didn't recognize them. Safe.

We huddled together, panting. It wasn't quite as dark when they were near me, though it was more a feeling than reality.

Cold pinched my cheeks. I reached up and touched wetness.

Tears.

One of the other girls sniffled.

"What's your name?" I asked.

"It's—" The green-eyed girl started panting. Moonlight illuminated her panic-filled eyes. "I don't know!"

"I don't either!" the other girl cried. "I don't know my name!"

I tried to think of my own, poking for memories.

Pain.

I didn't know how old I was. Or where I was from. It hadn't been a fluke before. I really couldn't remember. "I don't know anything either!"

We gasped and cried, huddling closer. Their warmth felt familiar, like we'd done this a hundred times before. Slowly, it soothed me. I tried reaching into my mind to draw out some memories.

"Ouch." I cringed.

"What's wrong?" asked the dark-haired girl.

"Every time I try to remember something, my head hurts."

"Me too," said the green-eyed girl.

"And me," sniffled the other.

"Then what do we remember?"

"Run," said the dark-haired girl. "We're running, but I don't know from what."

"Is that how we got into the field?" I asked.

"Maybe." Her voice shook. "*Run* was all I remembered. When I woke, it was the only thing in my mind."

"*Hide*," I said, thinking back. "That's what I remembered. We must hide. From a bad man." I rubbed my temple. "Or woman? From someone very bad."

Just the shadowy memory made tears pour down my face. My shoulders shook. The trembling traveled down my arms and legs until my entire body quaked.

I couldn't remember who we were hiding from, but my body remembered. Hiding from evil. Bad. *Bad, bad, bad.*

The green-eyed girl threw her arms around me. "Hey, hey, calm down. It'll be okay."

I gasped through my sobs and realized I'd been saying *bad* out loud. I didn't believe that it'd be okay—not really—but her words made me feel a little better.

"What do you remember?" I asked.

"FireSoul," she whispered. "We are FireSouls."

I gasped and jerked out of her arms. "No, we're not. We can't be."

I might not have remembered my own past, but some knowledge of the world still seemed to be intact.

FireSouls were bad. Even the word sent a shiver of panic through me.

Run, *hide*, and *FireSoul* were my only memories? That couldn't be. In my mind, I poked for the biggest, most important pieces of information. I wanted to know something.

What came was that I lived in a world full of magic. Thoughts burst in my mind. "I'm one of the Magica—you two feel like Magica as well."

I could feel their power now that I tried. Could smell it and taste it. The green-eyed girl's power felt like water on my skin and smelled like flowers. Tasted like vanilla. The dark-haired girl was just as powerful. Her magic felt like soft grass beneath my feet and smelled like fresh laundry. It tasted sweet, but I couldn't place it.

"Magica?" the dark-haired girl asked.

"Magica can create magic!" the green-eyed girl said, excitement in her voice. "I remember now. But I don't remember what kind I am. Witch, or sorcerer, or... mage."

"Or shifter, demon, or fairy," I added as the memories flowed back. "But they aren't Magica. They are supernaturals like us, but they don't use magic the same way we do. But they know about us. Unlike humans. The Great Peace keeps us hidden." It came back to me in pieces. Though we lived alongside humans, the Great Peace—the most powerful bit of magic ever created—hid us from human eyes. It took the powerful spells of hundreds of Magica and shifters to create the Great Peace. "Humans can see us but not our magic, which we shouldn't use around them anyway."

"Right, I remember now," the dark-haired girl said.

"I feel your power too. But you don't feel evil," I said. "Not like a FireSoul would feel."

"We're not evil," the green-eyed girl said. "We haven't killed...I don't think. But I do remember that we're FireSouls. I know it."

"Everyone hates FireSouls," I whispered. They were the bogeyman because they stole the magical gifts of others by killing the original owner. Was *I* the bogeyman? Me and these two girls? Had I killed another Magica to steal his gift? Wouldn't I remember something as terrible as that?

"Is that why we're hiding?" the dark-haired girl asked. "Are we hiding from the Order of the Magica and the Alpha Council?"

"No," I said, though the two supernatural governing organizations would be after us if they knew we were FireSouls. "We're hiding from someone worse. But if we really are FireSouls, we can't tell anyone. They'll throw us in prison."

"We are FireSouls," she said. "When I woke, I knew it. It was my memory. As strong as yours."

I swallowed hard, remembering how strong that urge to hide had been. I'd woken confused, but when the dark-haired girl had said *run*, it had burst back into my consciousness.

"Are we really FireSouls?" the dark-haired girl asked. "I don't feel like a FireSoul. I don't feel evil."

I didn't either. I felt hungry and cold. My stomach growled and I shivered. If only I had something to eat. If only I was warm. I wanted it so badly.

A strange feeling tugged at my middle. As if there were a string tied around my waist that pulled me to the left. A sense of food and warmth flowed from the invisible string.

"There's food and shelter nearby," I said. "I feel it."

"Treasure," whispered the green-eyed girl. "You can sense treasure."

Treasure. Of course I could sense food and shelter. I coveted them. They were treasure to me right now.

I was a FireSoul. That was proof.

FireSouls were given that name because they shared a piece of a dragon's soul, though no one knew how it had happened. If dragons still existed, they were hiding. But legend said that all magic descended from dragons. FireSouls somehow shared a part of their soul.

That's why we could steal powers and find treasure. Dragons were covetous. They coveted treasure of all varieties—including the powers of others. The greatest treasure of all could only be obtained through death.

"We can find what we need with our dragon-sense," said the green-eyed girl. "If we want it badly enough, it becomes treasure. Then we follow our sense to it."

Was that how we were supposed to survive? Become hungry enough to find food and then steal it?

I looked down at my ragged dress and skinny body. The only thing I had of value was the necklace, and even that was probably almost worthless. It didn't look like I had a lot of choice right now. If I had parents, I had no idea who they were or how to find them.

My throat tightened. Did I have a mom and dad? Where were they? I pushed through the pain in my mind, trying to remember. But nothing came. Just blinding agony. I slumped against the other girls.

"Are you okay?" one asked.

"Yes." I pushed thoughts of parents away and focused on surviving. "If we use our dragon sense, we have to be careful."

If we were caught, we would be thrown in the Prison for Magical Miscreants. It was a cold, dark, terrible place, I remembered that. A shiver ran over me. My own personal bogeyman. In the corner of my mind, it felt like someone had once threatened me with that prison, but when I poked at the memory, the blinding pain came again. Why didn't I learn? I needed to quit poking at my personal past.

"We need names," I said.

"Yes. I hate not having one," said the dark-haired girl.

The green-eyed girl looked up at the sky. "I will be Phoenix. After the constellation. Call me Nix."

I liked that. Naming ourselves for something bigger gave me hope. I looked up too. A cluster of bright stars caught my eye. I didn't know what in my past had taught me the constellations, but I was grateful for it. "I'll be Cassiopeia. Call me Cass."

The green-eyed girl looked up and sighed. "You took the best ones."

I giggled, the sound surprising me.

"I'll take Delphinus," she said finally. "But it'll be Delphine. And you can call me Del."

"Okay. Del and Nix." They both looked so different. Panic gripped my throat as I realized that I didn't know what I looked like. I pulled my hair around. Red. "We look nothing alike. I don't think we're related by blood, even though we're all FireSouls."

They were rare from what I remembered, but I didn't recall the gift being genetic.

"We're sisters now," Nix said. "Because we're all we've got. I don't remember my parents."

"Me neither." Del sniffed back tears.

"We'll find them." I closed my eyes and focused on the idea of parents. I wanted them more than anything, so I should be able to find them.

But the magical string didn't tie itself around my middle. I thought harder, reaching into my mind, pretending it was a book I could flip through.

Agony pierced my skull.

I retreated, gasping.

"I tried to find them," I said. My parents were lost to me. My throat tightened and tears burned. "I don't think I know enough about them. I could imagine food and find that. But people are harder, I think."

"We'll find them somehow," Del said.

I nodded, trying to hope but finding it hard.

"We can only use our dragon sense to find food and other things we need," I said. "No killing for other powers." I didn't want to be a murderer, no matter how much power it got me.

Nix nodded. "I don't want to be a monster."

"Me neither," said Del.

"If another supernatural asks how we can find things, we say we are Seekers," I said.

The green-eyed girl smiled. "That's a good idea. Camouflage ourselves."

"Exactly." Seekers were a type of supernatural who could find things. As long as we didn't kill and steal powers, we could use our ability to find treasure and just say that we were Seekers.

"Do we have other powers we can use?" Del asked.

"I don't know," I said. If it was about me directly, I couldn't seem to remember. "FireSouls can be other types of supernaturals as well. You both feel magical to me."

Nix closed her eyes. I felt her power surge against me like water lapping at my skin. The taste of vanilla burst on my tongue, and her flower scent filled my nose. Her hands began to glow. She cupped them in front of her.

Eventually, a small match appeared in her palms.

"You're a conjurer," I said as my power swelled within me.

"Not a very good one," Nix said. "I wanted to conjure a fire for warmth."

I listened with half an ear as the power in my chest grew. It felt like it was in response to hers, spurred on by what she had. I embraced it, though I didn't understand it, and held my arms out. The magic pulsed within me, roaring to be released. I raised my palms to the sky and let it go.

An enormous fireball shot from my palms, throwing me back onto the ground as it roared into the sky. It burned away the tops of the trees and exploded into the night. Orange flames surged through the air, burning my skin.

Panic rose in my chest as I scrambled to my feet. We were trapped. Del and Nix looked at me with horrified eyes.

"I don't know what happened!" I said. The sky above me continued to burn, though the forest around us was untouched. "People will see the flame! We have to hide!"

Del lunged for me. She enveloped me in her arms and grabbed Nix, pulling her into the hug. A second later, the ground fell out from under me.

We collapsed to the ground a moment later. It was colder here, the wind stronger. I climbed to my feet. We were on a mountain looking down on the field below. Fire roiled in the air above it, a beacon of magic. But at least it wasn't lower. The animals and the people would be safe.

"We were in a valley," I said as I turned to Del. "And you can transport."

Del's wide eyes met mine. "Apparently. It was instinct. I followed it. And thank magic for it. What did you do down there?"

I looked down at the field that was lighting up the night. It would draw people. We were fine on the mountain for a little while because we were so far away, but we needed to get out of here soon.

"I didn't mean to light it all on fire," I said. "When Nix conjured the match, I felt like I could create a match too. So I let my power out."

"You're a Mirror Mage," Nix said. "You borrowed my conjuring power."

"A strong one," Del said.

"Too strong. I couldn't control it."

Mirror Mages weren't rare or very dangerous, from what I recalled. They could reflect back the magic of any supernatural that they were with. But it was just temporary, and the other supernatural got to keep their powers the whole time. From what I remembered, if Mirror Mages didn't use the borrowed gift right away, they could use it later. But it was a one shot deal. I could have held on to the conjuring gift I'd borrowed from Nix, but I'd only have been able to use it once.

In a way, Mirror Mages were a tiny bit like FireSouls because they used the powers of others. But they weren't very dangerous because they couldn't keep the magic or replicate it more than once.

I turned toward the valley. The fire was starting to dissipate, but it was still an unnatural spectacle, the sky alight with flame.

"I could have killed us if I hadn't pointed my hands to the sky," I whispered. "I'm dangerous."

"I think you need to practice," Del said.

"Or not use my power at all." Tears pricked at my eyes. Why was I like this?

"Let's not worry about that now," Nix said. "We should get out of here. Let's find food and shelter."

I nodded and blinked the tears away. "Okay. Let's go."

We set off along the mountain ridge, following the magical string tied around our waists. I was tired and scared, but at least I had my *deirfiúr*. My sisters.

But as I walked, the most horrible thought occurred to me. Had I been born a Mirror Mage, or had I killed someone for this gift?

CHAPTER ONE

Ten Years Later
Temple of Murreagh
Deep Beneath Western Ireland

"Cass! Answer me, damn it. Are you hurt?" Nix's voice echoed quietly from the pendant around my neck.

"Gimme a sec," I wheezed as I shoved the huge rock off my leg and scrambled behind a big boulder. Pain radiated from my shin, but nothing felt broken, thank magic. I didn't have time to deal with it anyway. A nasty looking shadow demon was currently trying to blow my head off. As long as my limbs were mostly functional, I was good to go.

A blast of magic blew apart the stone over my head.

I ducked and rubble bounced off my shoulders.

Damn demon!

When it stopped, I peered over the boulder at the demon who guarded the altar in the middle of the underground temple. It'd taken me nearly six hours to get through the enchantments that led to the temple. Fire charms, moving rocks, an awful riddle—the whole lot. Real Indiana Jones stuff, but I didn't have the cool hat.

After all that, it seemed like it should be smooth sailing. But no, this treasure was protected by a shadow demon. Who was apparently very displeased with my presence.

His skin was dark gray, his powerful body clad in simple pants and a shirt. He was basically human-shaped, except for the exceptionally bulky arms and the narrow black horns that came out near his temples and ran back along his skull. Dark eyes glinted maniacally through the dust in the air.

Though big, he was dwarfed by the subterranean temple that housed the Chalice of Youth, my current assignment. The chalice sat on an altar behind the demon, gleaming gold. Graceful columns supported the soaring stone ceiling, each carved in the shape of a different long-forgotten goddess. The only light came from eerie torches that lined the walls. The air was stagnant, permeated by the scent of smoke that wafted from the shadow demon.

"Do I send backup?" Nix asked through static.

"No. I've got this." I didn't usually need my friends to step in and save my butt on a job, but it gave me the warm fuzzies to know they were willing. "You're breaking up, Nix. Too much magic from the demon. I'm turning you off now."

Strong magic, like the kind the demon was throwing, usually interfered with the comms charm that hung around my neck. Something about the magical signature overpowering the puny charm that fueled my necklace.

I usually worked alone, but sometimes—okay, always—a riddle enchantment stumped me. At that point, Nix was there to back me up via a quick call through my comms charm. But now that she'd gotten me through the riddle that had opened the main door to this temple—Why does a dragon cross the road?—I no longer needed her help.

"Fine, don't—" More static broke up Nix's voice.

"If I'm not out in an hour, remember that I hate lilies," I said. "Worst funeral flower."

"But—"

I touched the silver charm around my throat, and its magic went dormant. Only the sound of the shadow demon's breathing echoed in the chamber.

It was time to get this over with. I was starving, and this was my last gig before the long weekend. My leg screamed as I pushed myself to my feet. *Breathe through the pain. It's just bruising.*

I drew my obsidian blades from the sheaths strapped to my thighs and stepped out from behind the boulder. Torchlight reflected wickedly off the black volcanic glass. Lefty and Righty, I called them—not nearly regal enough names for their power—but I'd never been good at clever names.

"Time to go back to hell, fella," my voice echoed in the stone chamber. "The devil says he's missin' ya."

The shadow demon laughed, his dark gray skin absorbing the light. Fine, it was a little corny, but I was tired.

The demon raised his hand to throw another blast of magic at me. I flung Righty at him, dodging the whoosh of magic that he managed to get off before my blade sunk into his arm.

Perfect hit. Ten points.

He roared in pain as heat seared my shoulder through my leather jacket.

Oh, so he wanted to play that way? With heat as well as wind? I thought wistfully of blasting him back with a reflection of his own power. His magic manifested as burning smoke. I'd give him a flaming tornado.

Except that was the problem. My magic was too powerful for me to control. I just blew shit up if I tried. I didn't want to draw attention to myself, so I didn't use my power. But I didn't hide that I was a Mirror Mage—strong supernaturals could tell I had magic. If I didn't use it often, my magical signature appeared weak to those strong enough to sense others' powers.

So I'd gotten really good with weapons.

I pricked the back of my hand with Lefty before immediately throwing the blade at the demon's heart. My blood ignited a spell that would call its twin back to me.

As Lefty hurtled toward the demon, Righty pulled itself out of the demon's arm and flew through the air toward me. As long as I was quick—which I usually was—I always had a dagger at hand.

I reached up and snagged Righty as I kept an eye on the dagger that zoomed toward the demon. He used magic to blast it away.

"That's all you've got?" he roared.

I dove behind the nearest column, a stone warrior woman in a flowing cloak, both of her hands gripping swords.

A guardian. Of me, I decided.

I swiped my dagger over the small amount of blood welling on the back of my hand so that my other blade returned to me.

The demon roared again, his muscles bulging beneath his thin shirt as he drew his arms back to throw twin blasts of magic at me. All supernaturals had different gifts and his seemed to be throwing blazing blasts of smoke that blew things apart like a grenade.

The smoke blast hit my guardian column. Her bottom half blew apart, rock and debris flying across the temple. With an enormous cracking sound, the guardian crashed to the ground. The stone floor vibrated beneath my feet. Dust filled the air until I could hardly see.

Guilt ate at me over the damage done to such an ancient place. Don't worry about that now. Fix it later. I jumped onto the guardian, who was now lying on the ground in several large pieces, all lined up in a row. I raced across her skirt, jumping from piece to piece until I was right above the shadow demon.

I leapt for him.

He looked up at the last moment, his eyes widening. He twisted and Lefty sank into his meaty shoulder. With a roar, he threw me off him. I skidded across the floor, then groped my way behind the top of the fallen column. He was strong, both in magic and form, and his magic smelled ancient. Like dust. I'd bet he was an old demon.

"Blades?" he yelled. "You come at me with blades? Use your magic and give me a real fight!"

"What? You bored? Been guarding this tomb a long time, eh?" I said as I flung Righty at him.

It sank into his chest, nearly a perfect shot at his heart. Or at least, where I figured a shadow demon's heart might be.

He yanked it out and said, "You have no idea."

I swallowed hard.

Missed his heart, I guess.

Quickly, before he could fling the dagger, I called it back to me. Righty pulled itself out of the demon's hand and flew home.

The demon didn't startle, nor did he look weakened by the dark blood leaking from the wound in his chest. Old and strong, like I'd thought. Even if I hadn't hit his heart, he should at least be incapacitated. But this one was different. He wasn't even winded from the blade that had sunk six inches into his chest.

"Well? Won't you give me a real fight? You are one of the three. Strong enough to fight, but you don't."

My heart tried to climb into my throat. "What does that mean?"

The three? Did he mean me and my *deirfiúr*? How could he know about Del and Nix?

"What do you mean?" I screamed when he didn't answer quickly enough.

"You don't use your powers." He threw another blast of magic at me. Blazing smoke blasted away my column barricade, and I scrambled back.

He wouldn't use his powers either if it meant getting locked up in the Prison for Magical Miscreants. As long as I didn't use them, I could pretend that I was nothing but a low-strength Mirror Mage and have a lovely life where no one tossed me in prison.

The shadow demon threw another blast of fiery smoke. It plowed into the ground in front of me. The stone floor exploded. The blast threw me backwards. Pain streaked through me. My entire front felt singed, pierced by small pieces of shattered stone. A cough tore through my lungs and I blinked blindly, my throat and eyes burning.

I could barely see, and he kept throwing those damned blasts of smoke at me, driving me ever backward. I just had to get him to lay off for a sec. Then I could question him.

Through the dust, I could make out his hulking form approaching. It was risky, but I threw each of my blades in quick succession, hoping to incapacitate but not kill.

The thud of a body collapsing sounded. The blasts of power stopped coming.

I climbed to my feet and limped toward the form sprawled on the ground. The stone bit into my knees when I dropped beside him. My blades protruded from his chest, one embedded in each pectoral. His breath strangled in and out of his lungs, but he wasn't dead. I grasped his rough shirt and shook him.

"What do you know about me?" I said.

"What"—he coughed—"you are."

"But—"

His lips parted, and I snapped my mouth shut, frantic to hear what he had to say.

"FireSoul."

I stumbled back, my stomach twisting. Chills raced over me. How could he know that? No one knew that but my *deirfiúr*.

"I'm a Mirror Mage." My voice came out hardly louder than a whisper. I tried again, louder, fear choking my throat. "I'm a Mirror Mage!"

Panic welled in me, and I crawled back to him, reaching for his shirt again, desperate to shake answers from him.

His eyes were dimming, their gleaming black light turning a dark gray. A great breath shuddered out of his lungs, followed by stillness.

The light faded from his eyes, and his body disappeared. My blades, no longer embedded in a chest, clattered to the floor.

"No!"

My heart threatened to break my ribs. I hit the ground, frustration and fear beating in my chest.

The demon was gone. Not dead—you couldn't really kill a demon—just send them back to whatever hell they'd originally come from. Normally very neat and tidy. Except this one had information about me, and my blades had been too accurate. The demon had seemed so strong when my first blade had found its mark. I'd wanted to question him more. This was what happened when I freaked out. Like a bull in a china shop. And it was the main reason I could never use my magic.

My breath echoed too loudly in my ears. Think, think. How could the demon have known that I was a FireSoul? Was it because this job was in Ireland, my homeland? At least, what I assumed was my homeland, given that I could speak Irish and had red hair.

One option was so terrifying I couldn't even poke it with my mind. It was the bogeyman that lurked at the corner of my memories. Whenever I pressed too hard, it leapt up, bringing with it a splitting headache and adrenaline like nobody would believe.

I had to get out of there. Talk to Nix.

Quickly, I grabbed my blades, shoved them into their sheaths, then climbed to my feet. I limped to the altar, pain singing up my leg, and grabbed the golden chalice. It's magic sang beneath my palm, an unsteady beat that indicated this was old magic. The perfect age for selling. There were other priceless objects too, no doubt tributes to the gods carved onto the columns.

My fingers itched to pocket a couple, namely a golden dagger encrusted with rubies and a strange hexagonal blade that looked wickedly sharp on all sides. Despite my terror, covetousness surged within me. My hand trembled as I reached toward the golden dagger. Just one touch. I wouldn't take it.

No.

I sucked in a deep breath and clenched my fist. Not mine. Not mine. Like an addict resisting a fix, I dragged my gaze away from the glitter.

With a shaking hand, I pulled a small black rock out of an inner jacket pocket. My last transport charm. Like all magic that wasn't my own, they were expensive and hard to come by. Del could make them because she could transport, but her power was limited and they commanded a lot of it, so she couldn't make them often.

I should use the charm only in emergencies.

But this sure felt like a heck of an emergency.

I threw the stone to the ground. It shattered and a glittering silver cloud rose in front of me. I stepped into the sparkling stuff and envisioned my home. Magic grabbed me around the waist and threw me through the ether.

Ancient Magic is available on Amazon.

AUTHOR'S NOTE

Thanks for reading *Demon Magic!* As with all of my books, I included historical and mythological elements. If you're interested in reading more about these parts of the book, read on. At the end, I'll talk a bit about why Del and her *deirfiúr* are treasure hunters and how I try to make that fit with archaeology's ethics (which don't condone treasure hunting, as I'm sure you might have guessed). I spoke about this in the Author's Note in *Magic Undying*, so a lot of it is the same as in that Author's Note. But it's important stuff, so I wanted to include it here for anyone who might have missed it in *Magic Undying*.

So, the history and mythology in *Demon Magic!* This book starts out with a fun one—the wreck of the Klondike Gold Rush steamboat *A.J. Goddard*. I could talk your ear off about this boat. I won't, though. Promise. But just a little bit of info, since it is just so cool.

Contrary to what fiction tells us, most shipwrecks don't survive in good conditions underwater. Lake

Laberge is actually part of the Yukon River in a section where the river widens. The water is so cold and fresh that the wreck was in *amazing* condition. Almost fully complete, just the way I described it. But that's not the only cool thing about the *A.J. Goddard*. By far, one of the neatest elements is that this boat was carried over the Chilkoot Pass by men, women, and mules in the mountains of British Columbia. Carried over the mountains! Amazing. But if they wanted to reach the gold fields as soon as the ice melted on the Yukon River, that was the fastest way to do it.

And the boots that I mentioned on the lakebed? Those boots are really there. The boat's engineer, Julius Stockton, took them off as the boat was sinking and jumped overboard to swim to shore. Fortunately, he made it and wrote about the wrecking event. If you want to know more about the A.J. Goddard or see some amazing pictures, just Google it or check out my Pinterest page at www.pinterest.com/HiLinseyHall. There's even a National Graphic documentary about the boat.

The other cool historical element in this book is Dinorwic Quarry in north Wales. This is the location of the dragon cave, the Morgen, the Coblynau, and the crazy mining carts. Dinorwic Quarry is a real quarry that was in operation for about three hundred years. It's abandoned now—slate hasn't been mined there for decades—but it's pretty much just as I described it, with the massive ramps and old railroad track for the mining carts. The track disappearing off the cliff because of a rockfall is even there. The lake is actually situated farther away, though. You don't have to cross it to reach the ramps.

However, I put the lake there because I wanted to include some Welsh mythological figures. Morgens are beautiful, immortal women who live in the water and lure men to their doom. Morwena, the Morgen in this book, was somewhat more helpful than a usual Morgen, but only because she was grateful that Del and Roarke had gotten rid of the Afanc. Afanc are Welsh water monsters who also lure people to their doom, and Morwena wasn't pleased that the Afanc was stealing her business. Coblynau are Welsh mining gnomes, but they are usually helpful and not quite so murderous (though they can be blamed for rockfalls). However, that doesn't make for a fun trip up a mountain, so my Coblynau were given the power to kill with a touch, a power that they normally don't possess.

That's it for the historical influences in *Demon Magic*. However, one of the most important things about this book is how Del and her *deirfiúr* treat artifacts and their business, Ancient Magic. This is the part of the Author's Note that is written in *Magic Undying*, so if you've read that, this'll be a repeat. But it's important enough that I like to include it in all my books. My conscience wouldn't rest otherwise.

As I'm sure you know, archaeology isn't quite like Indiana Jones (for which I'm both grateful and bitterly disappointed). Sure, it's exciting and full of travel. However, booby-traps are not as common as I expected. Total number of booby-traps I have encountered in my career: zero. Still hoping, though.

When I chose to write a series about archaeology and treasure hunting, I knew I had a careful line to tread. There is a big difference between these two activities. As much as I value artifacts, they are not treasure. Not even the gold artifacts. They are pieces of our history that contain valuable information, and as such, they belong to all of us. Every artifact that is excavated should be properly conserved and stored in a museum so that everyone can have access to our history. No one single person can own history, and I believe very strongly that individuals should not own artifacts. Treasure hunting is the pursuit of artifacts for personal gain.

So why did I make Del and her *deirfiúr* treasure hunters? I'd have loved to call them archaeologists, but nothing about Cass's work is like archaeology. Archaeology is a very laborious, painstaking process—and it certainly doesn't involve selling artifacts. That wouldn't work for the fast-paced, adventurous series that I had planned for *Dragon's Gift*. Not to mention the fact that dragons are famous for coveting treasure. Considering where the *deirfiúr* got their skills from, it just made sense to call them treasure hunters.

Even though I write urban fantasy, I strive for accuracy. The *deirfiúr* don't engage in archaeological practices—therefore, I cannot call them archaeologists. I also have a duty as an archaeologist to properly represent my field and our goals—namely, to protect and share history. Treasure hunting doesn't do this. One of the biggest battles that archaeology faces today is protecting cultural heritage from thieves.

I debated long and hard about not only what to call the heroines of this series, but also about how they would do their jobs. I wanted it to involve all the cool things we think about when we think about archaeology—namely, the Indiana Jones stuff, whether it's real or not. But I didn't know quite how to do that while still staying within the bounds of my own ethics. I can cut myself and other writers some slack because this is fiction, but I couldn't go too far into smash and grab treasure hunting.

I consulted some of my archaeology colleagues to get their take, which was immensely helpful. Wayne Lusardi, the State Maritime Archaeologist for Michigan, and Douglas Inglis and Veronica Morris, both archaeologists for Interactive Heritage, were immensely helpful with ideas. My biggest problem was figuring out how to have the heroines steal artifacts from tombs and then sell them and still sleep at night. Everything I've just said is pretty counter to this, right?

That's where the magic comes in. The heroines aren't after the artifacts themselves (they put them back where they found them, if you recall)—they're after the magic that the artifacts contain. They're more like magic hunters than treasure hunters. That solved a big part of my problem. At least they were putting the artifacts back. Though that's not proper archaeology, I could let it pass. At least it's clear that they believe they shouldn't keep the artifact or harm the site. But the SuperNerd in me said, "Well, that magic is part of the artifact's context. It's important to the artifact and shouldn't be removed and sold."

Now *that* was a problem. I couldn't escape my SuperNerd self, so I was in a real conundrum. Fortunately, that's where the immensely intelligent Wayne Lusardi came in. He suggested that the magic could have an expiration date. If the magic wasn't used before it decayed, it could cause huge problems. Think explosions and tornado spells run amok. It could ruin the entire site, not to mention possibly cause injury and death. That would be very bad.

So now you see why Del and her *deirfiúr* don't just steal artifacts to sell them. Not only is selling the magic cooler, it's also better from an ethical standpoint, especially if the magic was going to cause problems in the long run. These aren't perfect solutions—the perfect solution would be sending in a team of archaeologists to carefully record the site and remove the dangerous magic—but that wouldn't be a very fun book.

Thanks again for reading (especially if you got this far!). I hope you enjoyed the story and will stick with Del on the rest of her adventure!

ACKNOWLEDGMENTS

As always, thank you, Ben, for everything you've done to support me in this career. Thank you to Andrew Meredith for writing to me and suggesting Wales as an excellent place for a book, and thank you to Sue Hackling for translating the Welsh name of the town of Cwm Y Ddraig (Valley of the Dragon).

Thank you to Jena O'Connor and Lindsey Loucks for various forms of editing. The book is immensely better because of you! And thank you to Rebecca Frank for the beautiful cover. You really bring Del to life.

Thank you to Tannith Strugnell for the name of the band that graces Connor's T-shirt. Thank you so Aisha Panjwaneey for catching typos.

The Dragon's Gift series is a product of my two lives: one as an archaeologist and one as a novelist. Combining these two took a bit of work. I'd like to thank my friends, Wayne Lusardi, the State Maritime Archaeologist for Michigan, and Douglas Inglis and Veronica Morris, both archaeologists for Interactive Heritage, for their ideas about how to have a treasure hunter heroine that doesn't conflict too much with archaeology's ethics. The Author's Note contains a bit more about this if you are interested.

GLOSSARY

Afanc - A Welsh water monster who lives in the depths of the northern lakes and drowns those who come into the water.

Alpha Council - There are two governments that enforce law for supernaturals—the Alpha Council and the Order of the Magica. The Alpha Council governs all shifters. They work cooperatively with the Alpha Council when necessary—for example, when capturing FireSouls.

Blood Sorceress - A type of Magica who can create magic using blood.

Coblynau - A Welsh goblin who lives in quarries and kills those who trespass.

Conjurer - A Magica who uses magic to create something from nothing. They cannot create magic, but if there is magic around them, they can put that magic into their conjuration.

Cwm Y Ddraig - Valley of the Dragon, a town full of supernaturals in north Wales.

Dark Magic - The kind that is meant to harm. It's not necessarily bad, but it often is.

Deirfiúr - Sisters in Irish.

Demons - Often employed to do evil. They live in various hells but can be released upon the earth if you know how to get to them and then get them out. If they are killed on Earth, they are sent back to their hell.

Dragon Sense - A FireSoul's ability to find treasure. It is an internal sense that pulls them toward what they seek. It is easiest to find gold, but they can find anything or anyone that is valued by someone.

Elemental Mage – A rare type of mage who can manipulate all of the elements.

Enchanted Artifacts – Artifacts can be imbued with magic that lasts after the death of the person who put the magic into the artifact (unlike a spell that has not been put into an artifact—these spells disappear after the Magica's death). But magic is not stable. After a period of time—hundreds or thousands of years depending on the circumstance—the magic will degrade. Eventually, it can go bad and cause many problems.

Fire Mage – A mage who can control fire.

FireSoul - A very rare type of Magica who shares a piece of the dragon's soul. They can locate treasure and steal the gifts (powers) of other supernaturals. With practice, they can manipulate the gifts they steal, becoming the strongest of that gift. They are despised and feared. If they are caught, they are thrown in the Prison of Magical Deviants.

The Great Peace - The most powerful piece of magic ever created. It hides magic from the eyes of humans.

Hearth Witch – A Magica who is versed in magic relating to hearth and home. They are often good at potions and protective spells and are also very perceptive when on their own turf.

Magica - Any supernatural who has the power to create magic—witches, sorcerers, mages. All are governed by the Order of the Magica.

Morgen - A Welsh water monster. She is a beautiful woman who lures men to their death in the water.

The Origin - The descendent of the original alpha shifter. They are the most powerful shifter and can turn into any species.

Order of the Magica - There are two governments that enforce law for supernaturals—the Alpha Council and the Order of the Magica. The Order of the Magica govern all Magica. They work cooperatively with the Alpha Council when necessary—for example, when capturing FireSouls.

Phantom - A type of supernatural that is similar to a ghost. They are incorporeal. They feed off the misery and pain of others, forcing them to relive their greatest nightmares and fears. They do not have a fully functioning mind like a human or supernatural. Rather, they are a shadow of their former selves. Half-bloods are extraordinarily rare.

Seeker - A type of supernatural who can find things. FireSouls often pass off their dragon sense as Seeker power.

Shifter - A supernatural who can turn into an animal. All are governed by the Alpha Council.

Transporter - A type of supernatural who can travel anywhere. Their power is limited and must regenerate after each use.

Warden of the Underworld - A one of a kind position created by Roarke. He keeps order in the Underworld.

ABOUT LINSEY

Before becoming a writer, Linsey Hall was a nautical archaeologist who studied shipwrecks from Hawaii and the Yukon to the UK and the Mediterranean. She credits fantasy and historical romances with her love of history and her career as an archaeologist. After a decade of tromping around the globe in search of old bits of stuff that people left lying about, she settled down and started penning her own romance novels. Her Dragon's Gift series draws upon her love of history and the paranormal elements that she can't help but include.

Copyright 2016 by Linsey Hall
Published by Bonnie Doon Press LLC

Linsey@LinseyHall.com
www.LinseyHall.com
https://twitter.com/HiLinseyHall
https://www.facebook.com/LinseyHallAuthor

BONNIE
DOON
PRESS

ISBN 978-1-942085-14-0